Secret
Clique

MARILYN KAYE

BOOKS

NEW YORK • TORONTO • LONDON • SYDNEY • AUCKLAND

RL 5.5, 008–012
SECRET CLIQUE
A Bantam Skylark Book / May 1999

ISBN 0-553-48685-3

With affection,
to the students of Rondout Intermediate School,
Accord, New York

Secret Clique

one

In the hallway at Parkside Middle School at 8:15 A.M. on a Monday, Tasha Morgan gazed around at the clumps of students talking, slamming locker doors, and generally hanging out. Then she spoke with an air of gloom.

"This school is *so* boring."

Her best friend, Amy Candler, considered this statement. "Why do you say that?"

"Think about it," Tasha explained. "Every day is exactly the same. In precisely three minutes the warning bell will ring, and we both know what's going to happen. Everyone will stop socializing and go to their homerooms. Two minutes after that, the final bell will ring. Then my teacher will clap her hands three times, which is the signal to stop talking. And it's always three times—never two, never four. What's the first thing *your* teacher does?"

"Ms. Weller raps on her desk with this paperweight she has," Amy told Tasha. "It's in the shape of the Statue of Liberty."

"And I'll bet she does that every day," Tasha said. "Right?"

Amy nodded. "Every day."

"And then she calls roll, right? And after roll call comes the daily announcements from the principal's office."

"But those announcements aren't the same every day," Amy pointed out.

"They're *practically* the same," Tasha argued. "Club meetings, special events, and sports. Right?"

Amy had to admit that the daily announcements pretty much followed that pattern.

"And what comes next?" Tasha asked.

Amy thought. "Ms. Weller usually has something to pass out. Notes to take home, forms to fill out, that sort of thing."

"Then I'll bet she collects something she passed out the week before," Tasha went on. "After that she'll tell you to study. Or if she's in a good mood, she'll give you permission to talk quietly. Right?"

"Right," Amy acknowledged.

"It's the same routine in my homeroom," Tasha said. "Then the bell rings, and we go to first-period classes. Then we go to second-period classes. Then to—"

"I get your point," Amy interrupted. "Okay, every day is pretty much the same. But I think all middle schools are like that."

"That doesn't make me feel any better," Tasha said. "Wouldn't it be nice if something different happened once in a while?"

"Remember when that horror movie was filmed here?" Amy reminded her. "That was pretty different."

"That was *then*," Tasha sighed. "This is now."

Amy grinned. "Cheer up. Life is full of surprises."

"For *you*, maybe," Tasha said. "But you're different."

"Thanks, I really need the reminder," Amy said sarcastically. "And would you mind lowering your voice?" The warning bell rang, and everyone started moving. "Meet you here after homeroom?" she asked Tasha.

Tasha nodded. "Don't we *always* meet right here after homeroom?"

Amy laughed at her friend's sorrowful tone. But she had to admit that Tasha was right. A day at Parkside Middle School was predictable.

On this particular morning, Amy slipped into her seat an instant before the final bell. She had about ten seconds to greet homeroom friends before Ms. Weller banged her Statue of Liberty on the desk. Then the teacher called the roll, with perfect timing. Less than a second after Adam Ziegler said "Here," the intercom crackled.

"Good morning, all Parkside students and staff," Dr. Noble began. "May I have your attention for the morning announcements?" The principal didn't wait for an answer. And her announcements held no surprises.

"The Chess Club, the Spanish Club, and the yearbook staff will be meeting after school today. On Wednesday evening, the Parkside basketball team will be playing Turner Middle School, and the Girls' Chorus will be performing at the Sunshine Square minimall on Sunday afternoon."

There was a warning about overdue library books, a reminder about recycling cans and bottles in the cafeteria, and the results of an election held the Friday before to replace a student council member who had moved away. "In the special election for ninth-grade class treasurer," the principal announced, "the winner is Lori Kessler."

Amy didn't belong to the Chess Club or the Spanish Club, and she wasn't on the yearbook staff. She already knew about the basketball game, since her boyfriend, Eric, was on the team, and she made a mental note to check out the Girls' Chorus if she happened to find herself at the minimall on Sunday. The election didn't mean anything to her. Seventh-graders didn't vote in a ninth-grade election, and she didn't even know who Lori Kessler was.

But someone in her homeroom was clearly pleased with the election results. Jeanine Bryant let out a little squeal of delight and clapped her hands. What's she so happy about? Amy wondered. She glanced at her neighbor, Linda Riviera, who happened to be Jeanine's best friend. A flicker of annoyance crossed Linda's face; apparently she wasn't particularly happy about the election. Or maybe it was Jeanine's reaction to the news that displeased her.

Amy had to admit she was mildly curious about this.

As her archenemy since first grade, Jeanine was always a subject of some interest. Linda and Jeanine were pretty much joined at the hip, and Linda usually followed Jeanine's lead in every way. Obviously, something had changed in that relationship.

Amy had to wait until Ms. Weller had distributed PTA flyers to take home, and until forms distributed the previous week had been collected, and until the teacher had given permission for quiet conversation, to satisfy her curiosity.

Amy turned to Linda and got right to the point. "Why does Jeanine care about who's going to be ninth-grade treasurer?"

Linda responded sullenly. "Lori Kessler's in that clique."

Now Amy understood. There were a lot of cliques at Parkside—cliques made up of athletes, or computer nuts, or boys who hung out at the video arcade, or girls who hung out at the mall. There was a clique made up of kids who had taken over the school literary magazine and the Arts Club, and there was a group who dressed in punk style and dyed their hair wild colors. As someone who wasn't much into group activities, Amy was never quite sure who was in which clique.

But she knew the clique Linda was referring to. She'd seen Jeanine with them on the school steps on recent mornings. They were popular kids, mostly ninth-graders, with only a few seventh- and eighth-graders allowed to hang out on the fringe of the group. Amy didn't know much about this bunch, but they clearly thought they were pretty special.

That explained Jeanine's response to the news, and Linda's reaction to Jeanine's response. Jeanine now considered herself part of this clique, and she'd dumped Linda as her constant companion. Linda was hurt.

Cheer up, Amy wanted to tell her. Jeanine's not worth it. But she couldn't do that because that kind of conversation could be dangerous. It could lead to friendship, and sharing secrets. It could lead to Linda's learning more about Amy than Amy wanted her to know. More than Amy wanted *anyone* to know.

Almost anyone. One of the exceptions to that rule was waiting for her in the hall when the bell rang. Tasha's homeroom was just across the hall, and their first-period classes were side by side, so the girls always walked together.

Linda was just behind Amy as she came out the door. "See you, Amy," she called. "Hi, Tasha."

Tasha watched Linda's departing figure in surprise. "Why is she being so friendly all of a sudden?"

"She needs friends," Amy replied. "Jeanine blew her off for the clique that hangs out on the front steps." She kept her voice low as she spoke, since Jeanine was walking just a few yards in front of them.

"I still can't believe she's running around with *them*," Tasha marveled. "You see those girls she's walking with? They're ninth-graders. That's Blair Cavanaugh, she's a cheerleader. And the girl with the blond hair, that's Kristy Diamond, she was a runner-up for Miss Young America."

"Don't be so impressed," Amy advised her. "They can't be all that cool if they're letting Jeanine hang out."

"Oh, you just have a problem with Jeanine," Tasha said.

"Can you blame me?"

Tasha cocked her head thoughtfully. "Well, considering that she probably put poison in your soup at the National Essay Competition, I guess not."

"Jeanine Bryant is bad news," Amy stated flatly. "I'm glad she's got all those new friends. Maybe now she'll be less interested in me."

The morning passed in its usual way—math, geography, English. Lunch was mystery stew, along with some beige things that looked like fries but tasted like cardboard. There was nothing new about that. After lunch, Amy had French.

The French teacher smiled as Amy came in. "*Bonjour, Amy.*"

"*Bonjour,* Madame Duquesne," Amy replied.

She passed other students who were frantically cramming. Madame Duquesne always gave quizzes on Mondays. Amy took her seat in the back of the room, opened her textbook, and pretended to study. She didn't *need* to study, of course—she'd completed the assignment the night before in five minutes. She wondered how long it had taken the other students to learn the past tenses of eight irregular verbs. More than five minutes, that was for sure. It was at times like this that Amy appreciated being . . . different.

A pretty girl with long blond hair slipped into the seat next to her. She leaned over to see what Amy was looking at in the textbook. "Are we supposed to know that stuff?" she asked in dismay.

"That was the assignment," Amy reminded her. "Past tenses of the verbs on page a hundred and twenty-two."

"I thought we were supposed to learn the verbs on page a hundred and twenty-one!"

"We had to learn those verbs for the test *last* Monday, Tracee. Don't you remember?"

Tracee Bell sighed. "I guess not." She opened her book. It was too late, though. The bell rang, and Madame Duquesne went into the Monday routine. She said *"Bonjour"* to the class and told them to clear their desks. Then she opened her briefcase and took out the quizzes.

As the tests were passed out, Amy glanced at Tracee with sympathy. Tracee had failed this class twice, so she was the only ninth-grader taking seventh-grade French. This didn't particularly embarrass or bother her. She was always cheerful and friendly. In fact, she was one of the few members of the front-steps clique who said "Hi" to Amy when she passed by.

Even though this was her third time around, the poor girl was still having trouble in French. Madame Duquesne had assigned Amy to be Tracee's conversation partner for the five minutes of "free expression" they had every day at the end of the class. Unfortunately, after they'd asked each other "How are you?"

there wasn't much else Tracee could say, so making conversation wasn't easy.

Today was no different. When Amy asked her, *"Comment ça va?"* Tracee responded with a gaping yawn and nothing else. At least the yawn provided Amy with a topic for conversation.

"Est-ce que tu es fatiguée, Tracee?"

Tracee looked at her blankly. "Huh?"

They weren't supposed to speak any English, so Amy opened her French-English dictionary and pointed to the definition of the verb *se fatiguer*—to be tired.

"No kidding," Tracee said. "I'm wiped out."

"En français, Tracee," Amy reprimanded her. *"Oui, je suis . . ."* and she pointed to the word again.

"Oui, je suis fatiguée," Tracee repeated obligingly. She looked at Madame, who was conferring with two other students on the opposite side of the room. Immediately Tracee shifted to English.

"I was at a sleepover last night, and I didn't shut my eyes till two! Normally I'm not allowed to stay at someone's house on weeknights, but this was a special occasion. Melissa's home!"

"Qui est Melissa?"

Tracee actually managed to understand the question. "Melissa Mitchell! You remember, she was in that terrible car accident at the start of the school year. She's been in the hospital six months, and this is her first day back at school."

Amy tried to translate part of that into French. *"C'est son premier jour—"* but then the bell rang. Melissa Mitchell, Melissa Mitchell . . . she couldn't come up with a face, but the name was definitely familiar.

The name became even more familiar as the day wore on. In the halls, in the cafeteria, in the locker room, half the school was talking about the return of Melissa Mitchell. Dressing in the locker room after phys ed, Jeanine went on and on about her.

"She almost *died,* you know. She was in a coma for *months,* and she had like a hundred operations on her head. But you won't believe it when you see her—she's just as great-looking as before. You can't even see any scars on her! And the crowd is *so* happy to have her back, everyone's giving her welcome-home parties." Jeanine's voice dripped awe and respect. Apparently this Melissa was a major member of the clique.

By the end of the school day, Amy was tired of hearing about the great Melissa Mitchell, and she hoped

Tasha wouldn't talk about her all the way home. She was really happy to find Eric waiting just inside the exit when she and Tasha were leaving school. If he walked home with them, there would be other topics of conversation.

"Don't you have basketball practice today?" she asked him.

Eric shook his head. "Coach has a toothache. I'm waiting for Kyle. We're going to shoot baskets."

Tasha's eyes narrowed. "Here or at home?"

"Haven't decided. Why?"

"Because the last time Kyle came over, he ate the whole cheesecake Mom made for a company dinner. Mom was *not* happy, remember? So just keep him out of the kitchen."

Eric responded in the authoritative big-brother voice he could use only with Tasha. "Don't give Kyle a hard time, Tasha. He's got problems today."

"Like what?" Amy asked.

"Well, he lost the election for ninth-grade treasurer, for one thing. To Lori Kessler. I still can't believe she's going to be treasurer. I had math with her in seventh grade and she could barely add."

"Maybe she's improved," Amy suggested.

"It wouldn't matter," Eric told her. "I warned Kyle that no one can beat that clique in an election. They have total control over the student government. And now Kyle's about to get kicked off the basketball team."

"How come?" Tasha asked.

"He's never been a good player," Eric explained. "He tries hard, but he just doesn't focus very well. It didn't matter much before, when we were losing, but now that we have a shot at the regional championships, the captain thinks he's becoming a liability. And Kyle knows it." He eyed Tasha sternly. "So if the poor guy wants a little cheesecake, don't bug him."

A group of girls passed by, and one of them, tall and dark-eyed with short hair, called out, "Hi, Eric."

"Hi," he responded. "Welcome back."

Now Tasha looked at her brother with new respect in her eyes. "You know Melissa Mitchell?"

"She went with Spence Campbell last year," he said. "He brought her to a few basketball parties."

Amy gazed at the girl's back as she moved through the doors with her friends. So *that* was the famous Melissa Mitchell. She was certainly pretty, and she moved with confidence, but somehow, from the way people spoke about her, Amy had expected to see someone more . . . extraordinary.

"Hi, guys." Eric's pal had arrived. Both Tasha and Amy turned to him with big smiles. "Hi, Kyle!" they exclaimed in unison.

Kyle Osborne gave them a forlorn grin. "Okay, don't overdo it, I'm not that depressed."

They started out the door. A crowd was gathered at the bottom of the steps. "What's going on?" Kyle asked.

"It's the Melissa Mitchell Fan Club," Eric said. "Remember when she used to go with Spence?"

Kyle winced. "Can we not talk about Spence, please?"

"Spence is the basketball captain now," Eric explained to the girls. They edged past the group and onto the sidewalk. "Where do you want to practice?" Eric asked Kyle. "Around back on the playground?"

"Nah, I don't want to run into anyone from the team. Can we go over to your place?"

"Sure," Eric said, ignoring Tasha as she mouthed the word *cheesecake*. Some of the kids from the steps, including Melissa, passed them en route to the street corner, and Kyle eyed Melissa appreciatively.

"Wow, six months in the hospital sure hasn't hurt her," he commented. "She's still a babe."

"Forget it, Osborne, she's out of your league," Eric said good-naturedly.

"I don't get it," Amy whispered to Tasha as they walked behind the guys. "What's so special about her?"

"She's just, you know, cool," Tasha replied lamely.

The special cool one was a little ahead of them. The group surrounding her had dwindled to three girls, and they seemed to be walking a pace behind Melissa, as if she was royalty or something. They didn't go down to the corner crosswalk. Instead, they got ready to cross in the middle of the busy street.

Just as Melissa stepped off the curb, Amy saw something out of the corner of her eye—a car, making a left and heading their way. Melissa had her head turned to speak to one of her friends and couldn't see the car. Amy's mind went into fast forward. In an instant she was able to calculate the speed and the distance of the vehicle, and she screamed, "Watch out!"

Kyle had noticed the car too. He leaped forward, grabbed Melissa's arm, and jerked her back. The driver must have realized what was about to happen, because the car swerved at the last minute.

Everyone surrounded Melissa and Kyle, with cries of "Are you okay?" and "Kyle, you're a hero!" Only Amy saw what happened to the car.

The driver had stopped, and she could see him reach for the door to get out. Then, suddenly, the car lurched forward, turned, and plowed directly into a tree.

And burst into flames.

two

Amy raced toward the burning car, ignoring Eric's cry for her to stop. She knew why he was calling to her: Her special talents didn't make her impervious to fire. But she thought she might be able to move fast enough to get the man out of the car before it was engulfed in flames.

Fortunately, she wasn't required to risk her own skin. The driver had been halfway out of the car when it stopped the first time. When it hit the tree, he was thrown clear.

He couldn't have been badly hurt. He got up right

away and watched in horror as his car burned. Then he too joined the crowd that surrounded Melissa.

Someone must have called 911. Amy could hear the sirens off in the distance, and within seconds an ambulance, a fire engine, and two police cars arrived on the scene.

Amy watched as one police officer began talking to the driver of the car while another pushed his way through the crowd to reach Melissa. Two paramedics jumped out of the ambulance and pulled a stretcher from the back.

The stretcher wasn't necessary. Tasha emerged from the crowd and told Amy that Melissa seemed to be fine.

"She's hysterical, but I think that's just from the shock," she added.

"You can't blame her for that," said a familiar voice. Amy turned and saw Tracee. "She's just recovered from one car accident and she almost gets hit by another car! Thank goodness for your friend, whoever he is."

"Kyle Osborne," Amy told her. "He's a nice guy. But that car wouldn't have hit Melissa anyway. The driver stopped just in time." She paused. "But you know what was weird? The way the car suddenly started moving again and then plowed right into that tree."

"I'll tell you something even weirder," Tracee said. "You, running to that car when it burst into flames."

Tasha gasped. "Amy, you did that?"

"I guess that was kind of stupid," Amy admitted.

"And I can't believe how fast you can run," Tracee continued. "I've never seen a girl run that quickly."

Amy avoided Tasha's eyes. "Yeah, well, you know . . . when you're in a panic, the adrenaline flows."

Luckily, Tracee didn't ask for more of an explanation. She moved to join the select group of friends who were still huddled around Melissa. The fire was out, so the fire trucks left, and so did the ambulance. The crowd was beginning to disperse, and Amy could see Melissa. She seemed to have calmed down considerably, but she was still clinging to Kyle.

"Are you sure you shouldn't go to a hospital?" Kyle was asking her.

"No, no, I'm all right now," Melissa told him, but her voice was quivering.

She certainly looked fine to Amy—there wasn't a mark on her. But why would there be? The car hadn't touched her. Everyone was making an awfully big fuss over nothing. It hadn't even been a close call. Amy felt sorrier for the poor guy who had lost his car and was now being questioned by the police.

Still, Melissa probably was a little unnerved. And now she was looking up at Kyle, and her eyes were shining.

"You saved my life," she murmured in awe. Personally, Amy thought that was something of an exaggeration, but Kyle blushed and looked pleased.

A police officer came toward them. "I hope you're going to put that man in jail," Tracee said to him.

The police officer shook his head. "No, he doesn't appear to have done anything wrong. Did anyone here actually see what happened?"

"I did," Amy said. "The driver wasn't going very fast, and he swerved to avoid hitting anyone. I think the girls just stepped off the curb without looking." She frowned. "What I don't understand is why the car went into that tree."

The police officer shrugged. "There are a lot of possible explanations. The driver might have hit the accelerator accidentally. Or maybe there was some sort of faulty wiring. In any case, *he's* lucky to be alive."

"So is Melissa!" one of her friends piped up.

The police officer smiled. "Can I give you a ride somewhere, miss?"

"Well, I *am* a little shook up," Melissa admitted. Immediately her friends began begging her to come home with them. But Melissa was still looking at Kyle, her eyes wide with gratitude.

"You want to come with us?" Kyle asked her. "We're going over to Eric's to shoot some hoops."

Melissa beamed at him. "Yes."

That was how Amy found herself being taken home in a police car with Eric, Kyle, Tasha, and Melissa. It was a new and interesting experience. Unfortunately, Amy's mother just happened to be home, and she just happened to be looking out the window when the police car pulled up.

Amy was barely out of the backseat when Nancy Candler came flying across the lawn toward her. "Amy! What happened? Are you all right?"

Everyone started talking at once, and words like *car, accident,* and *fire* were jumbled together. This didn't reduce the panic in Nancy's eyes. Amy took her arm firmly and tugged.

"Come on, Mom, let's go inside." To the others, she called, "I'll be out in a few minutes."

"We'll be on the driveway," Eric called back to her.

By the time they got into the house, Nancy was breathing more easily. Once she realized that no harm had come to her daughter, she sank into a chair at the kitchen table and demanded to hear the whole story. Amy complied.

". . . And then the car burst into flames, and I—"

"You—what?" Nancy asked suspiciously.

Amy fumbled. "I, uh, called 911." There was no point in getting Nancy all upset again. "The police gave us a ride home."

"I was so scared when I saw that police car," her mother said, sighing.

"Did you think I tried to rob a bank or something?" Amy joked. But Nancy wasn't in a joking mood.

"No, I thought someone had tried to kidnap you."

Any other kid in the world would have accused her mother of being paranoid, but not Amy. Because the notion that she might have been kidnapped wasn't so far-fetched.

There were people out there, somewhere, who knew all about her. Who knew she'd been created in a laboratory from genetically superior material. Who knew there were eleven others exactly like her. DNA replications. Clones.

Those people, that secret organization, had been responsible for Project Crescent, on which Nancy Candler had worked twelve years ago as one of the project scientists. She and the others had believed they were conducting research to prevent genetic disorders. It wasn't until they realized that the organization's purpose was to create a master race, a species of people with superior skills who could take over the world, that they knew the project had to be abandoned.

Not wanting to destroy the infant life-forms they'd created, the scientists had sent them, the Amys, all over the world for adoption as normal children. Nancy Candler had taken one home to raise as her own daughter. And that was how Amy Number Seven had become Amy Candler.

Nancy had passed Amy off as her own daughter. And not until several months ago had Amy discovered the truth about her origins. It had been mind-boggling, but now she no longer thought of herself as a freak.

Instead, she considered herself someone special. Some-one who happened to have superior senses, superior strength, and superior intelligence. In essence, she was perfect. The perfect human. The perfect clone. It was a huge secret to keep, but she managed to keep it—from everyone but Tasha and Eric.

Nancy and the other scientists had thought they'd deceived the organization into thinking that the clones had been destroyed in the laboratory explosion. But in the past few months, events had convinced Amy and her mother that the organization knew of the clones' continued existence. And they wanted to get their hands on these gifted, talented, physically and mentally superior twelve-year-old girls.

Amy couldn't be sure whether the other Amys were being pursued. She'd come into contact with only two of them so far. Or maybe she'd met more in New York at the National Essay Competition the month before. But she couldn't be sure. She'd woken up one day to find herself in a hospital with other Amys, all of whom were being tested and experimented on. But now it ap-peared that the experience had been a hallucination caused by a drug that Jeanine had put in her soup. Or maybe not. It was all still a mystery. Amy's life was full of mysteries.

She watched as her mother made a cup of tea. Nancy seemed calm now. It was ironic, in a way. Amy was stronger and smarter than the average twelve-year-old, so Nancy really had less to worry about than an ordinary parent. But then, ordinary girls weren't as valuable as Amy. So maybe Nancy had *more* to worry about.

All Amy knew was that she didn't particularly want to think about any of this right now. Her friends were outside on the Morgans' driveway, and she wanted to be with them. Well, she wanted to be with Tasha and Eric. Kyle was okay too. Amy couldn't think of Melissa as a friend, though.

"Mom, I'm going out, okay?"

Nancy nodded, and Amy ran outside. The Morgans lived just next door, in the same condominium community. She found Tasha sitting on the ledge that bordered the carport. Melissa was on the opposite side of the driveway, watching Kyle try to take a basketball away from Eric.

"How come you're not talking to Melissa?" Amy asked as she joined Tasha on the ledge.

Tasha gave her a slightly abashed grin. "She makes me nervous."

"Nervous! Why?"

"She's just so—so *cool*. It's kind of scary."

Amy tried not to smile. She knew that superconfident people could be intimidating. But scary? That was a little extreme. "Come on, it's rude to leave her standing alone while Eric and Kyle are playing." She slipped off the ledge, and Tasha followed.

Melissa didn't seem to object to their company, but she didn't take her eyes off Kyle. "Isn't he amazing?" she crooned.

Amy knew Melissa couldn't be referring to his basketball game. Eric was practically giving the ball to Kyle, and he still couldn't take it away.

"So brave," Melissa went on. "Running out into the street like that to save me. Do you think he's cute?"

Amy tried to examine Kyle objectively. He wasn't very tall, and he was stocky, but he had a sort of cuddly teddy bear look. "Yeah, I guess he's cute."

"I'll bet he's the kind of guy you can count on," Melissa said.

That was probably true. Amy didn't know Kyle all that well, but he'd always seemed like the reliable type.

But she could also see why the basketball team couldn't count on him. Kyle had finally managed to take the ball, and he tried for a basket. His aim was completely off, and the ball didn't even hit the rim.

"Try it again," Eric urged. "And *look* at the basket."

Kyle took another shot. This time the ball didn't even hit the backboard.

Amy gave Melissa a sidelong look, hoping Kyle's lack of athletic expertise wouldn't discourage her interest in him. Amy was pleased to note that Melissa didn't appear to be that shallow. The pretty girl even tried to make Kyle feel better about his poor performance by finding something else to blame it on.

"It's the ball," she announced, looking at it where it had fallen. "I think it's a little flat."

"It felt okay to me," Eric said. He went over to the ball and picked it up. "Well, maybe not. It *is* a little soft." Amy beamed at him, pleased to see that Eric could be sensitive to Kyle's feelings too.

"And you'll be a lot better in a real game, with a crowd and cheerleaders," Melissa added.

Kyle didn't think so. "I do worse when people are watching," he said. "And cheerleading doesn't do anything for me."

Melissa sighed. "That's because of the head cheerleader, Kelly Marcus. One of my best friends, Blair Cavanaugh, is on the squad, and she says Kelly makes them do the dumbest routines. Blair would be a much better head cheerleader."

Amy and Tasha looked at each other and shrugged. Neither of them knew any of the cheerleaders, so they had no opinion.

"Who's hungry?" Tasha asked.

Kyle's eyes lit up. "Cheesecake?"

"No, but I think we've got cookies," Tasha told him.

That didn't excite Kyle. "Nah, I should practice some more. Spence is going to be watching me at the game tomorrow night. He'll be looking for any excuse to cut me from the team."

A shadow crossed Melissa's face. "You don't have to listen to *him*."

"I *wish*," Kyle said fervently. "But he's captain, and Coach lets him run the show." He eyed Melissa with increasing interest. "So, you and Spence don't hang out together anymore?"

"I hate him," Melissa said. "Do you know what he did while I was in the hospital? He started going with another girl."

Amy was puzzled. Melissa had been in the hospital for six months, and she and Spence certainly hadn't been engaged to be married. Still, she didn't say anything. The hostility in Melissa's eyes was a little unnerving.

Kyle didn't seem bothered by it, though. "Um, I was wondering . . . if maybe you're coming to the game tomorrow night . . . we usually go out for ice cream afterwards. To celebrate, if we win."

"And to feel better if we don't," Eric added.

Kyle spoke a little nervously. "I thought, I mean, if you don't have anything else to do, you could come with us."

Melissa flashed him a big, beautiful smile. "I'd love to," she said.

Kyle was clearly pleased. A deep red blush crept over his face. Then he turned to Tasha. "Are those cookies you mentioned homemade?"

Tasha nodded. "Chocolate chip with nuts."

As they all started inside, Amy pulled Eric aside. "That was nice of you," she said.

"What?"

"Telling Kyle the ball was soft."

"I wasn't making that up," Eric told her. "It *was* soft.

I don't know how that happened, 'cause it was fine when we started playing."

"Oh. Well, maybe that really was the problem," Amy said. "And maybe Kyle will play better tomorrow night."

"Maybe," Eric echoed. But he didn't look optimistic.

The Parkside Rangers had been steadily improving all season, and attendance at the games had increased. Amy arrived alone—Eric had gone to the gym earlier for a warm-up, and Tasha was finishing an essay that was due the next day. But Amy found some classmates on the bleachers, so she could do her cheering with company.

Thanks to Eric, she was really starting to enjoy basketball. She liked the speed, the way the scores climbed so quickly and were continually being tied and then broken, especially when teams were equally matched.

Eric had a lot to do with the accumulation of points. Amy watched with pride as he darted around the other players and practically snatched the ball from their hands. More than half of his shots resulted in baskets.

Of course, if Amy had been out there playing, *all* the shots would have sailed cleanly through the net. Her extraordinary eyesight gave her perfect aim, and her strength meant that she could shoot a basket easily from the opposite end of the court. With her on the team, the Parkside Rangers would be the basketball champions of the world. But that was precisely why she didn't go out for team sports—or individual sports, for that matter. People would notice. And they would wonder how she could be that good.

Eric knew how. He knew she could beat him at everything, from footraces to computer games. Some girls wanted a boyfriend who was stronger, faster, and smarter than they were, but Amy wasn't one of them. It didn't bother her that Eric could never make the high grades she could, and it didn't bother Eric either. Amy hoped Melissa would appreciate Kyle's limited skills too.

As far as basketball was concerned, those skills were *seriously* limited. Kyle was doing very little on the court tonight, probably to avoid messing up badly. It had to be hard on him, knowing that Melissa was watching. Looking around, Amy spotted the ninth-grader with her special clique just a few rows down. Jeanine was there too. Amy hoped Melissa wouldn't invite *her* to join them for ice cream.

A cheer went up from the crowd on the other side of

the gym, the visitors' side. The Turner team was ahead, and there were only a few minutes left in the game. Within seconds, though, someone from Parkside tied the score.

Now Turner had the ball. Parkside played defensively, preventing the Turner guys from getting too close to the net. But they couldn't take the ball away from Turner. Then, with less than a minute remaining, Eric got his hands on the ball. But he was way too far from the net to be sure of getting a basket. He threw it toward a cluster of Parkside guys who were closer. To Amy's utter amazement, it was caught by Kyle.

Kyle looked stunned. Seconds remained, and there was no time for him to pass the ball. He threw it wildly in the general direction of the net.

From the second the ball left his hands, Amy knew that there was no way on earth that his effort would win any points for the Rangers. Rapidly calculating the angle, she could see that the ball would miss the basket by a mile.

And then the strangest thing happened. The ball changed direction—as if blown by a gust of wind—and slipped cleanly through the basket, just as the final buzzer sounded. Parkside had won the game. *Kyle* had won the game for Parkside.

The crowd went wild. The players looked stunned. Kyle stood frozen, his mouth open.

Amy waited outside the boys' locker room while Eric showered and changed. Melissa was there too, and she was very happy. "Wasn't Kyle wonderful?" she asked Amy.

"Yeah, wonderful," Amy said, but she still couldn't make any sense out of what had happened.

When Eric came out, he too was in a mild state of shock. "Did you see that?" he asked. "Was that weird, or what?"

"How did it happen?" Amy demanded.

"Beats me," Eric said.

Melissa spoke. "My mother would say Kyle had a lucky angel on his shoulder."

Eric grinned at her. "Well, I hope the angel stays there!"

three

3

On Sunday morning Amy woke up early. She stretched luxuriously and glanced over at the twin bed on the other side of her room. Tasha had stayed over and was still sleeping. Amy didn't try to wake her. It was nice having a few moments alone to collect her thoughts.

Thank goodness she wasn't having her nightmare much anymore, the one where she was trapped in a glass case with a fire raging all around her. When she was younger, the dream had been really frightening because it was so bizarre. Now she had the dream only once in a while, and she could deal with it because she knew what it meant. It was the memory of her rescue from the burning laboratory twelve years ago. Amazing that she could remember back that far. Well, maybe not so amazing. Like all her mental abilities, her memory was phenomenal.

She didn't need a phenomenal memory to recall the evening before, although she probably remembered more details than a regular person would. In this particular case, she didn't mind, because the memory was so pleasant. Eric had taken her and Tasha bowling.

It had been the first time for the two girls. The bowling alley was a ninth-grade gathering place. Seventh-graders weren't banned, but any seventh- or eighth-grader would feel a lot more comfortable in the company of a ninth-grader. And two other ninth-grade friends of Eric's had met them there—Spence Campbell, the basketball captain, and his girlfriend, Sarah Klein—so Amy and Tasha had entered with confidence.

Amy had caught on to bowling right away, careful not to show off too much with her perfect aim. She'd made only one big boo-boo, when she underestimated her strength and threw the bowling ball so hard it shattered one of the pins.

Everyone had been stunned. People at other lanes

had heard the crash and come over to see, and the manager of the place had walked down the lane to examine the damage. Lying in bed now, Amy could still feel her face going red with embarrassment. The manager had been bewildered. No one had ever busted a pin before, not even two-hundred-and-fifty-pound professional bowlers, he told them. It was impossible.

Amy had suggested that the pin must have been defective. The manager had been skeptical. But there'd been nothing he could do, since there was no other plausible reason.

Eric and Tasha had managed to keep straight faces, and Eric's two friends hadn't had any problem accepting Amy's suggestion. Still, Amy had been aware of some very strange looks coming from the other bowlers. She was glad that only her little group had actually witnessed the accident.

Their group was supposed to have been larger. But Kyle and Melissa had been no-shows.

"I guess they wanted to be alone," Tasha had suggested.

"They've been together nonstop since they met on Monday," Eric said. "Kyle and I were supposed to get together last night to watch the Lakers at a friend's house, but he didn't show up there either. Guess he was with her."

"Who are you talking about?" Spence asked.

"Kyle Osborne and Melissa Mitchell," Eric told him. "Don't tell me you haven't seen them in the halls. Talk about public displays of affection. They're inseparable. I haven't even talked to Kyle since the game."

"Oh, yeah," Spence said, and he looked distinctly uneasy. "Melissa can be, you know, kind of possessive." Amy remembered that Spence had a history with Melissa. She also recalled Melissa's words about Spence: that she hated him for going out with another girl while she was in the hospital. Was Sarah the other girl? Amy wondered.

Spence seemed to read her mind. "I know what Melissa says about me," he said defensively. "But for crying out loud, we only went out about three times before her accident. Now she's acting like I dumped her the minute she was out of commission!"

"And she's been giving me the most awful looks at school," Sarah added, shuddering. "It's starting to creep me out."

"At least she's a good influence on Kyle's playing," Eric said. "He's knocking himself out trying to impress her. That basket he made during the game was amazing."

Spence nodded, but he still looked uncomfortable. "Too amazing, if you ask me. It's like he knows some kind of weird trick throw."

"Wish he'd teach it to me," Eric said.

They'd gone back to bowling. Amy had managed to control her throws, *and* her aim, so that her score wouldn't be too spectacular. She'd won anyway.

The memory made her smile, and she stretched again. Then she sat up and tossed her pillow toward the other bed. "Wake up!" she ordered. "No sleepy-heads allowed!"

Tasha opened her eyes with a yawn. Pulling herself to a sitting position, she stretched, then winced. "My arm aches," she complained. "Those bowling balls are heavy."

"What do you want to do today?" Amy asked her.

"Nothing athletic," Tasha replied promptly.

"How about a movie?"

"Okay. Let's see one that's playing at Sunshine Square. I want to hear the Girls' Chorus."

"Oh yeah, they're singing at the mall," Amy recalled. "How come you're so interested in singing?"

"Marcy Pringle has a solo," Tasha told her.

"Who's Marcy Pringle?"

"A ninth-grader. She writes for *The Parkside News* with me."

"You mean *The Parkside Snooze*," Amy said, teasingly. That was what everyone called the weekly middle-school newspaper.

Tasha bristled. "It's getting a lot more interesting this term. We're doing serious stories now."

"Like what?"

"A couple of writers are investigating the ninth-grade treasury. There's a rumor going around that some of the student government officers have been taking money from certain organizations and stashing it away to pay for a ninth-grade dance."

"Better not let Melissa Mitchell hear about this," Amy warned her. "It's her crowd that runs the student government."

Tasha shrugged. "I don't think we'll be seeing much of Melissa anymore. It looks like she and Kyle are only into seeing each other."

Amy's mother agreed to take them to the mall, and the girls ran next door to get permission for Tasha. When they walked in, they heard Eric on the phone in the kitchen.

"Hey, man, where were you last night? Oh. You two are getting pretty exclusive, aren't you? You blew us off Friday night, too. Hey, don't get mad, I'm just saying, I hope you're not about to dump all your old friends for your new babe. We still on for this afternoon? Right, two o'clock. See ya."

"Was that Kyle?" Amy asked him when he came into the living room.

"Yeah. He was with Melissa last night. *And* the night before."

"They must be crazy about each other, if they want to spend so much time alone."

"Except that they weren't alone," Eric told her. "They were hanging with Melissa's friends. I can't believe Kyle really likes that crowd. They're such a bunch of snobs."

Tasha came running down the stairs. "It's okay, I can go."

"Where are you off to?" Eric asked.

"Sunshine Square," Amy replied. "Want to come?"

"No, I'm meeting Kyle at the Community Center. We're gonna try to get a pickup game going. I want to see if he can make another one of those awesome baskets, or if that was just a fluke."

It was around eleven when Nancy dropped the girls off at the mall. Checking a sign at the entrance, they saw that the Girls' Chorus would be performing in the central atrium at two-thirty, so they decided to see a movie first. At the triplex, they debated between a movie starring Leonardo DiCaprio (Tasha's heartthrob) and one with Matt Damon (Amy's personal favorite), and compromised happily on one featuring Brad Pitt.

Afterward they went to the food court, and after arguing the merits of Burger King versus Pizza Hut, they settled on Wendy's. At precisely two-twenty-five they went to the atrium.

They spotted the Girls' Chorus right away, distinctive in their white blouses and navy blue skirts. They were getting into place on risers that had been set up in the center of the open space. Passing shoppers glanced at them, but most kept on walking. Amy was glad she and Tasha had come. It would be hard on Marcy Pringle and the others if they didn't get an audience.

"Which one is Marcy?" Amy asked.

Tasha squinted. "I can't see her." She fumbled in her bag for her glasses and put them on. "Maybe she comes out after everyone else because she's doing the solo."

An extremely pretty girl with pink cheeks and long

blond hair did come out a bit later, but according to Tasha, she wasn't Marcy Pringle. "I don't know who that girl is," Tasha said.

Whoever she was, she turned out to be the soloist. The chorus director led the girls in a series of American folk songs. Amy thought the girl who sang the solo parts was really good.

Tasha wasn't as impressed. "Marcy sings a lot better," she said. "I wonder what happened to her."

A voice behind them answered the question. "She choked on a mushroom."

Both Tasha and Amy whirled around and found Melissa standing there. "What?" they asked in unison.

"Marcy Pringle was eating a pizza last night, and she choked on a mushroom," Melissa told them calmly. "So Kristy had to take her place."

"Is Marcy okay?" Tasha asked.

"I guess so," Melissa said. "But she can't sing for a while."

"I don't get it," Amy said. "How can anyone choke on a mushroom? Mushrooms are soft, and the ones on pizzas aren't very big."

Melissa shrugged. "I don't know. But it got stuck in her throat, and now her throat's all scratched."

"From a mushroom?" Amy was still puzzled. "That's hard to believe."

"Are you calling me a liar?"

"No, but—"

"I was there," Melissa went on. "At the Italian restaurant on Haygood. Marcy was with her parents. Can you imagine, on a Saturday night, with her *parents*? What a nerd. Anyway, a waiter had to use the Heimlich maneuver on her." She laughed softly.

Tasha looked shocked. "You think that's funny?"

"You should have seen her," Melissa said. "Anyway, it's nice for Kristy. She's been dying to be picked for a solo but the director always chooses Marcy."

"Is Kristy a friend of yours?" Amy asked.

"One of my best buds," Melissa replied. She gazed out past the girls, then looked at her watch. "He better not be late," she murmured to herself, tapping her foot impatiently.

"Who?" Amy asked.

"Kyle."

"He's playing basketball at the Community Center with my brother," Tasha told her.

"No, he isn't," Melissa said. "He's meeting me right here."

She was right. Seconds later Kyle ambled over to them. He smiled at Melissa and greeted her as if no one else was there.

Tasha corrected that impression immediately. "I thought you were supposed to meet Eric at the Community Center."

"Oh, yeah, right," Kyle said, looking a little abashed. "But just when I was about to leave home, Melissa called. I tried to call Eric but he'd already left. Tell him I'm sorry, okay?"

"I think *you* should tell him that, Kyle," Tasha said. "You know, you really shouldn't blow off old friends or you won't have any."

Melissa's eyes focused on Tasha. "Maybe Kyle doesn't need his old friends anymore. He's making new ones now."

"I guess you never went to summer camp," Tasha commented.

"What's that supposed to mean?" Melissa asked.

Tasha looked directly at Kyle. "There was this rhyme we used to sing. Something about holding on to old friends when you're making new ones. Do you remember that song, Amy?"

Amy nodded and recited the words. " 'Make new

friends, but keep the old, one is silver and the other gold.' "

Kyle looked away. Melissa responded for him. "This really has nothing to do with you, Tasha."

"I know that. I'm thinking about my brother."

"It's not his problem either," Melissa said. "Come on, Kyle." She linked an arm through his and pulled him away.

"She is so creepy," Tasha commented. "I wonder if that whole crowd is like that."

Amy refrained from reminding Tasha how impressed she'd been with that crowd just a few days earlier. "It's like Spence said last night," she said instead. "Melissa's possessive. I'll bet she was the kind of little kid who never let anyone else play with her toys."

Tasha grinned. "Remember how Jeanine acted in first grade, when someone undressed her Barbie? She went ballistic!"

Amy remembered. "Maybe that's why she fits in with Melissa's crowd." She looked at her watch. "Mom's picking us up in fifteen minutes."

"What do you want to do now?" Tasha asked.

Amy considered their options. "I know, let's stop at the bakery and get those cookies Eric likes, the ones with the M&M's in them. He's going to be in such a bad mood when Kyle doesn't show. Cookies might cheer him up."

Normally Tasha wasn't all that concerned with her brother's moods, but she agreed this time. The girls headed across the atrium. They were just walking under the awning that hung outside the bakery when an odd noise made Amy look up.

There was no time to call out a warning. She shoved Tasha out of the way, a microsecond before the awning came crashing down.

The two of them held on to each other and looked at the huge piece of metal that lay on the floor, right where they had been standing. Workers from the store came running out, and other shoppers gathered around.

"Are you all right?" a man in an apron asked anxiously.

Tasha was too shaken up to speak, but Amy answered for them. "We're okay. But I think you'd better do something about that sign."

"I don't understand this," the man said. "The metal awning was soldered onto the storefront. There's no way it could have broken off."

"Well, it *did*," Amy said. "And it could have crushed us both."

At that moment, the realization of what had happened hit Tasha and she burst into tears. The baker ushered her inside the store, and Amy was about to follow. But something made her look back toward the atrium. She could see Melissa and Kyle in front of a store. They seemed to be watching her. With a start, she realized Melissa was smiling.

Well, if that girl could laugh over someone's choking on a mushroom, she'd probably find the idea of someone's being crushed by a metal sign absolutely hysterical. Tasha was right. Melissa was creepy.

Tasha had recovered by the time Nancy came to pick them up. "Good heavens!" Nancy exclaimed as the girls climbed into the car. "What did you two buy?"

The girls were lugging bags and boxes full of every delicacy the bakery sold. The man had apologized to them by giving them tons of cookies, brownies, and cakes. Now Amy had to come up with an explanation. There was no way she could tell her mother what had really happened. Nancy was always worried about Amy. And even though this almost-accident had nothing to do with Amy's being a clone or with any kidnap attempt, she knew her mother would try to make some sort of connection.

Unfortunately, Amy's super-powers didn't make her supercreative. Tasha had the advantage when it came to being inventive. "We went into the bakery to buy some cookies," she told Amy's mother. "And it turned out that we were the one millionth customer! So the baker gave us all this stuff."

"How could both of you be the one millionth customer?" Nancy asked.

Tasha had anticipated that question. "We walked in at exactly the same time, so it was a tie."

Nancy glanced at Amy. "You're not getting your picture in the newspaper or anything like that, are you?"

"No, Mom," Amy assured her. "It's not that big a deal." She didn't like having to lie, but it was better than watching her mother have a nervous breakdown.

Back at the Morgans', Eric was grateful for the cookies, but he was definitely angry that Kyle had stood him up, and he was worried. "It's just not like him to act like this," he said. "I'm going to try calling him again." He went to the phone, but as he was about to pick it up, it rang.

"Hello?"

Amy saw him frown.

"Hello?" he repeated. Then he slammed the phone down.

"What's the matter?" Tasha asked.

"It's been ringing like that ever since I got home," Eric told them. "And when I pick it up no one's there."

"It's probably a wrong number," Amy said. "Or a computer mix-up at the phone company."

"Well, it's getting on my nerves," Eric muttered. "And it's weirding me out."

"Have a cookie," Tasha said comfortingly. "You'll feel better."

But it took almost two dozen cookies for Eric to start feeling better.

four

Eric was still in a foul mood at breakfast Monday morning. He shoved spoonfuls of cornflakes into his mouth without even tasting them.

"Could you pass me the butter?" his father asked.

Instead of picking it up and handing it to him, Eric pushed the butter plate across the table with such force that it would have fallen off if Mr. Morgan hadn't grabbed it just in time. And when Tasha asked him for the salt, he practically threw it at her.

"All right, what's your problem?" his mother demanded.

"Nothing," Eric muttered. The phone rang and he

leaped up to grab it. When it turned out to be for his father, he slumped back into his seat and looked even more irritated.

Both his mother and Tasha were now staring at him, so he relented and explained. "I called Kyle twice last night. The first time, I left a message with his mom, but he didn't call me back. The second time, he said he was busy and he'd call right back, but he didn't."

"Oh, give him a break," Tasha said. "He's got a girl-friend now. That can change a guy."

"So what?" Eric countered. "I've got a girlfriend, and I haven't changed."

He realized too late what he'd said. Now his mother was looking at him with more interest than he wanted. And Tasha was laughing like a hyena.

"Forget it," he growled, leaving the table. Upstairs in his room, as he gathered his books and other stuff for school, he mentally kicked himself for admitting in front of his mother that he had a girlfriend. Having a girlfriend was great, but coming out and saying it in front of parents was definitely uncool.

Not that he usually worried about being cool. That was one of the reasons he'd always avoided getting too tight with a clique, any clique. They all had their rules and regulations: what to wear, what to say, how to act. He needed more freedom than that. All his friends felt that way—or so he'd always thought. Could Kyle have really changed so much, so fast? Even if he was crazy about Melissa, did that mean he had to dump all his pals and start hanging out exclusively with a really obnoxious clique?

Apparently it did mean that. Because when Eric, Tasha, and Amy arrived at school, Kyle was on the front steps with Melissa, three other girls, and two guys. Eric knew both of the guys—Jeff Carmichael and Dean Patillo—and he didn't much care for either of them. Jeff was super-rich and always showing off the labels on his clothes. Dean didn't speak to you unless he was running for office.

One of the girls was Jeanine Bryant. She was jabbering away as usual, telling everyone about some triple-backwards-upside-down-inside-out flip she'd been practicing in gymnastics. "Coach Persky says that if I do this in competition, I'll blow away the judges," she bragged.

"That's nice," Melissa said in a bored voice. She looked at Kristy Diamond and rolled her eyes. Kristy giggled.

"But I'm thinking about dropping out of gymnastics and switching back to figure skating," Jeanine continued. "What do you think, Melissa?"

Melissa gazed at her through half-closed eyes. "I don't really *care*, Jeanine." Kristy and the others laughed, and Jeanine went red. Eric couldn't figure out what was going on, but there were a lot of things about girls he didn't understand. He looked at Kyle, who appeared embarrassed.

"Hey, Morgan," Kyle mumbled. "Sorry I didn't have a chance to get back to you last night."

Eric shrugged. "Yeah, whatever." Then, impulsively, he sat down on the steps. "How's it going?"

"Okay."

Eric was aware of Melissa and the others looking at him as if he didn't belong there, but he didn't care. He wasn't going to let them scare him off.

"We've got practice after school today," he said.

"Right." Kyle nodded. "I'll be there."

Melissa looked at him. "Kyle, you said you'd come over and fix my stereo today!"

"Oh, yeah, I forgot. . . ."

"You'd better be in the gym," Eric warned him.

"One great basket doesn't mean you can start skipping practice!"

Melissa glared at him. "You can't talk to Kyle like that! You can't order him around!"

"It's okay, Mel," Kyle said. "Eric and me, we go way back." He grinned. "I'll be there, Eric. And after practice, I'll fix the stereo."

Eric nodded with approval and some relief. Kyle might be under Melissa's spell, but he hadn't become her puppet.

Amy spoke to Kristy Diamond. "I heard you sing at Sunshine Square yesterday," she said. "You guys sounded great."

Kristy rewarded her with a smile. "Thanks!"

"How's Marcy Pringle?" Tasha asked her.

"Oh, she'll be okay," Kristy answered. "The doctor said she has to drop out of the chorus or she'll strain her voice."

"But that's awful!" Tasha exclaimed. "She's the best singer in the chorus!" Kristy didn't respond to that, but her narrowed eyes made it clear what she thought of Tasha's comment.

Amy looked at her watch. "The bell's about to ring,"

she announced. Eric followed them as they moved up the stairs. Just before the top step, Tasha stumbled and fell. She would have tumbled down the stairs if both Amy and Eric hadn't grabbed her.

"Look where you're going!" Eric warned.

"I was. What did I trip on?" Tasha asked in bewilderment, her face a bright pink.

"Your shoelaces came untied," Amy pointed out.

As Tasha knelt to tie the laces, Eric could see that Amy was pressing her lips together the way she always did when she was angry. "What's the matter?" he asked her.

"Those kids down there are laughing at Tasha," she whispered in his ear.

"I don't hear them," Eric said.

Amy looked at him pointedly, and he knew she was reminding him that she could hear a lot of things he couldn't. Actually, he was glad that normal human ears couldn't pick up the sound of muffled giggles from this distance. Tasha didn't need to feel any more embarrassed.

At least he was feeling a little better about Kyle now. Hopefully, Kyle wasn't going to hang out exclusively with his new crowd. But he was certainly spending a lot of time with them. At lunch that day, when Mac Krensky and Carl Stafford joined Eric at their usual table in the cafeteria, Kyle wasn't with them.

"Where's Osborne?" Eric asked his friends.

Mac made a face. "He's moved up to first class," he said, his tone thick with sarcasm.

"What's that supposed to mean?"

Mac jerked his head toward a table in the back, and Eric saw what he meant. Kyle was sitting with the two guys from the front steps, plus another couple of clowns from that crowd.

"Geez, why's he sitting with them?" Carl asked in an aggrieved tone.

"He's going with Melissa Mitchell," Eric informed him.

"Yeah, I know, but it's not like she's going to eat lunch with him," Carl said. There was an unwritten law at Parkside Middle School. Boys and girls never ate together in the cafeteria.

"Melissa's probably putting pressure on him to be friends with her friends," Eric explained. "Hi, Spence, what's happening?"

The captain of the basketball team didn't look happy as he joined them. "Any of you guys have a class with Sarah?"

"I do," Mac said. "Second period, biology."

"Was she in class today?" Spence asked him.

Mac thought for a minute. "No, she wasn't. Why?"

"She was supposed to meet me in the library before homeroom this morning and she didn't show up."

"Maybe she's sick and stayed home," said Eric.

Spence shook his head. "I talked to her last night and she was fine."

"Maybe it's one of those, you know, *girl* things," Carl suggested.

His comment pretty much killed that topic of conversation. The guys quickly switched to basketball talk, a much safer subject.

"You know, I almost feel sorry for Jeanine," Amy said as she speared some peas with her fork.

"You're kidding." Tasha paused in the process of trying to cut through a hunk of mystery meat. "Why do you feel sorry for *her*?"

Amy looked across the cafeteria at the table where her archenemy was sitting with her clique. "Well, Jeanine thought she was really in with that crowd. But I don't think Melissa wants her around. You heard how

Melissa talked to her this morning. And it looks like Melissa pretty much runs the show."

Tasha shrugged. "Serves Jeanine right for trying to push her way in. Besides, she's better off this way. You know, I thought maybe it was just Melissa who was strange. But after hearing them this morning, I think the whole clique is odd."

Amy studied the group. "They can't all be that bad. Tracee is okay. Not too intelligent, but sweet."

"They all look good from a distance," Tasha said. "But close up they're bogus." She twisted her head to take a look at the table. "What are they talking about now?"

"Oh, so you're still intrigued by them," Amy teased.

"Not intrigued," Tasha corrected her. "Mildly interested. After all, they're a pretty strange bunch. Strange people can be very interesting."

Amy agreed. She concentrated, but the noise of the cafeteria made it impossible for her to pick up the conversation. She could read one girl's lips, though.

"The girl with the short brown hair is talking about money," Amy told Tasha. "Something about how some reporter from the *Snooze* interviewed her and it made her nervous."

"That's Lori Kessler, the ninth-grade treasurer," Tasha said excitedly. "Wow, I'll bet she *is* scared. This is going to be a major scandal. They took money from the Chess Club and the literary magazine funds, and we've got proof. It's all going to be in the paper that comes out tomorrow."

"But you can't blame this on Lori Kessler," Amy pointed out. "She was just elected."

Tasha smiled smugly. "She was on the budget committee, so she was in on it. And so was Dean Patillo, the vice president of the student council. I'll bet some of them get suspended. At least they'll be kicked out of office. That clique's going *down*." She twisted her neck to look at them again. "What's Melissa telling Lori?"

Amy recited what she could read from Melissa's lips. "'Don't worry. I'll show you how to do it tonight.'"

"Do what?"

"I don't know. Now they're all giggling and nodding."

Tasha sniffed. "There's absolutely nothing Melissa can do. The editor's already brought the copy to the printer's." She rose from her seat. "I'm going to get some more milk. Want some?"

"No thanks."

It was when Tasha was returning with her milk that

the little accident happened. She tripped again, just as she had that morning—only this time she spilled a pint of chocolate milk all over her white T-shirt.

Amy jumped up. "Come on, we'll go to the rest room and wash it off."

"I'll never get it all off," Tasha wailed. "These stupid shoelaces! Why do they keep coming untied? I've been wearing these shoes for *ages*."

"Maybe the laces are weak," Amy suggested, though she'd never heard of such a thing. They passed Melissa's table on their way to the rest room, and neither of them missed the fact that the clique had witnessed the accident. All of them were looking at Tasha, and Kristy was laughing.

"I *really* don't like that girl," Tasha muttered as they went into the rest room.

"Which one?"

"Kristy. Just because I told her I thought Marcy is the best singer in the chorus, she's out to get me."

"Don't exaggerate. It's not like she made you trip," Amy said. "I can't remember—do you put cold water on chocolate stains or hot water?" In the process of helping Tasha, she got her own shirt soaked too.

It was still damp when she arrived at her French class

later that day. "What happened to you?" Tracee asked, looking at the wet spot.

"I was helping Tasha get chocolate milk off her shirt," Amy told her.

"Oh, was that the girl who tripped in the cafeteria?" Tracee asked. "Poor thing."

"Well, at least you're not laughing about it like your friend Kristy."

Tracee shrugged. "*I* don't hate Tasha."

Amy did a double take. Was Tracee implying that Kristy *did* hate Tasha? *Hate* seemed like an awfully strong word, given the situation.

From outside, the shrill sound of a siren could be heard. When it got louder, people began to look toward the window. And when the ambulance pulled up right in front of Parkside, kids ran to the windows to look out.

Amy joined them and saw paramedics jump out of the ambulance. They lifted a stretcher out from the back. "What's going on?" she asked the boy standing next to her.

"Don't know," he said. "Maybe there's been an accident."

The paramedics disappeared into the gym entrance.

A few seconds later they came out carrying someone on the stretcher.

"Who is it?" someone asked.

But they were too far away to see. Only Amy, with her superior vision, could make out the figure lying face up on the stretcher. "It's a girl with a cheerleader outfit on," she said.

"Yeah, it's Kelly Marcus. The head cheerleader. She broke her leg."

"Really!" Amy exclaimed. There was no way Tracee could have known that. "That's terrible."

"Is she a friend of yours?" Tracee asked.

"No, I don't know her at all."

"Then why did you say it's terrible?"

Amy was startled. "Well . . . it's terrible for *anyone* to break a leg. Don't you think so?"

Tracee shrugged. "I like to look on the bright side."

"What's the bright side of breaking a leg?"

Tracee smiled happily. "It's nice for Blair Cavanaugh. She was cocaptain of the cheerleading squad, and she never got along with Kelly. Now she'll be able to run the cheerleaders on her own."

Amy didn't know what to say. She was glad to see Madame Duquesne coming into the room; it gave her a chance to change the subject. "Are you ready for the quiz?" she asked Tracee.

"I don't think we'll be having a quiz today."

"But it's Monday," Amy said. Tracee didn't appear to be concerned.

After greeting the students with the usual *"Bonjour,"* Madame Duquesne did what she always did on Monday afternoons. She told the class to close their textbooks, and she opened her briefcase. The usual groan went through the room as they cleared their desks in preparation for receiving the tests.

But Madame Duquesne didn't take out a stack of tests. Instead, she stared at the contents of the briefcase, with a puzzled expression. As she began fumbling through her papers, the lines of perplexity on her face deepened.

"I must have left the tests in the teachers' lounge," she said. "Class, you may take out your textbooks and study while I go to get them."

Everyone in class began taking advantage of the extra study time. Amy turned to Tracee. "Hey, you're in luck, you can learn at least two of those verbs while she's gone."

But Tracee didn't bother to take out her book. She

pulled her cosmetics sack out of her purse and blithely began applying lip gloss. After that, she started filing her nails.

Amy watched her in surprise. Tracee wasn't too smart, but she usually *tried* to follow directions. Now she was acting like she didn't even care about failing a test.

As it turned out, the ninth-grader received another lucky break that day. Madame Duquesne didn't find the tests in the teachers' lounge.

"I don't understand this," she said. "It's as if they just flew away."

No one in class looked particularly sympathetic—in fact, there were even some smiles. Amy could appreciate that. She glanced at her neighbor, expecting to see her smiling too. But Tracee was still filing her nails.

In the gym after school, the basketball coach was not happy. "Where's Osborne?" he barked at no one in particular. "He can't afford to miss a practice."

That was exactly what Eric thought, and he was surprised not to see Kyle at the session. Hopefully, he'd be just a few minutes late.

The coach looked around, and his displeasure became

even more evident. "And where's Campbell? I can't believe this, your *captain*'s not even here! What kind of crummy team is this?"

No one took the coach's words to heart—that was just his way. But it *was* unusual for Spence to be late. He took his responsibilities as captain seriously. Usually the coach worked with them for half an hour and then Spence took over.

Coach put them through some running and passing drills. About thirty minutes later, Spence came running in.

"Why aren't you dressed?" the coach yelled. "You're supposed to be in charge here now!"

Spence began talking privately with him. Immediately, the coach's expression changed. He blew his whistle, the signal for everyone to gather around.

Now that he was closer, Eric could see that Spence was very upset. He soon learned why.

"You all know my girlfriend, Sarah," Spence said. "Sarah Klein. She's missing. She left for school this morning but she never made it here. Her parents have notified the police, and they're out looking for her." He flushed. "They've been asking me a lot of questions, too. They think I've got something to do with it, like, maybe Sarah and I were planning to run away together. But it's not true. I don't know where she is, and I'm just as worried as her parents. Anyway, that's why I'm late."

Coach spoke in an unusually gentle manner. "It's okay, Campbell. You go on home, I'll run the team through some more drills."

"Actually, I'd rather stay and practice," Spence said. "If I go home, I'll just hang around and think and worry and . . ." His voice cracked.

Coach became brisk. "Right," he said. "Go dress."

Spence went to the locker room, and the other guys on the team started talking. "Maybe we should form a search party," one suggested.

"Let the police handle this," Coach ordered them, but he looked worried.

Spence returned, and the coach left him in charge. "Let's do some free throws," Spence told the team, and they lined up to take a turn with the ball. Spence stood just behind Eric. "Where's Osborne?" he asked.

"I don't know," Eric said.

Kyle eventually showed up, sauntering into the gym in his street clothes. Eric couldn't believe how smug he looked.

"Where have you been?" Spence yelled. "You're over an hour late!"

"I had a meeting," Kyle told him.

"What kind of meeting?"

"None of your business."

"What do you mean, none of my business? I'm captain of this basketball team! If you can't be at a practice session, you need to come up with a better excuse!"

"Well, par-r-r-rdon me," Kyle drawled. "But maybe I don't need any practice sessions."

Eric was stunned, and so was Spence, who shouted, "Well, maybe we don't need you on this team!"

"Oh yeah?" Kyle went over to a player who was holding the basketball. He took the ball out of the guy's hands and threw it in the general direction of the basket.

It was a replay of last week's game. The ball didn't look like it was going to make it. Then it changed direction in midair and sailed cleanly through the net.

They all watched in awe—except for Spence.

"Look, Osborne! I don't care what kind of trick shots you've come up with. I'm in charge here, and I'm telling you, you're off the team!"

"I don't think so," Kyle said, glaring back at him.

Spence's eyes widened, and the color drained from his face. Kyle's attitude was no doubt compounding the distress Spence must be feeling about Sarah's disappearance. Spence turned and started walking out of the gym.

"Hey, where are you going?" someone called after him.

Eric looked up at the clock on the wall. "Practice is over," he said, but he was puzzled too. It wasn't like Spence to back down from an argument. But then, Spence had a lot on his mind.

The guys started toward the locker room. Eric ran to catch up with Kyle.

"Hey, what's the matter with you?"

"Nothing," Kyle said. He quickened his step and moved ahead to the exit. Eric followed him outside.

"Kyle! Kyle, wait!"

With a show of reluctance, Kyle paused and let Eric catch up. It was getting chilly, and Eric shivered in his basketball shorts.

"Look, man," he said, his teeth chattering. "Don't tell me nothing's going on! You're acting very weird."

Kyle said nothing at first. Finally, he spoke.

"Melissa says—" he began.

"Melissa says what? 'Act like a goof'?"

"Look, I'm playing good basketball now," Kyle burst out. "Isn't that enough for you?" With that, he turned and strode away.

Eric considered running after him, but he was freezing. He went back into the locker room.

"Where's Spence?" he asked one of the guys.

"He left."

"How could he shower and change that fast?"

The guy shrugged. "He didn't. I guess he just walked out of the building in his shorts and T-shirt. He didn't even pick up his jacket."

"But it's cold out there!" Eric exclaimed.

"Yeah, I know. I guess he's just too worried about Sarah to notice."

Eric tried to imagine how he'd feel if Amy disappeared. He knew he'd be frantic with worry too.

But he was pretty sure he'd remember to change his clothes.

five

"Are you going to say anything to Kyle?" Amy asked Eric as they approached Parkside the next morning. Eric had told her about the events the day before at basketball practice.

"It wouldn't do any good," Eric said gloomily. "He won't talk to me. I'm glad he's not in any of my classes. I really don't want to run into him today."

Amy looked toward the school. "Sorry, Eric, but you're going to be seeing him in about two minutes. He's sitting on the front steps."

The members of the clique were in their usual place. To Amy's sensitive eyes, they seemed to be huddling a little closer together than usual. Other students glanced at them as they made their way into school, but no one in the group seemed to be speaking to non-members. Even Tracee, who usually greeted Amy, didn't speak until Amy did.

"Hello, Tracee."

Tracee looked up and flashed a smile. "Hi, Amy." Then she returned to speaking in a low tone to Melissa. Amy caught a snippet of the conversation.

"Are we having a meeting tonight?" Tracee was asking Melissa.

"Of course," Melissa replied.

"They're having meetings now," Amy reported to Eric and Tasha once they were inside the school lobby. "Isn't that a little strange? I mean, cliques have parties, or barbecues, stuff like that. They don't have *meetings,* do they?"

"That does sound weird," Eric admitted. "Maybe they want to become an official school club so they can apply for funds from the student council treasury."

"In their dreams," Tasha scoffed. "Once everyone reads the article in the *Snooze*—I mean the *News*—today, those guys are history. At least, they won't be controlling the student government anymore."

The sound of three bells echoed through the school. This meant that a general announcement was about to be made over the public-address system.

"All members of the basketball team, please report to the principal's office before homeroom period."

Amy looked at Eric. "What's that all about?"

"I don't know. Maybe Spence told the coach he's kicking Kyle off the team and he wants to talk to the rest of us."

"But why would the principal want to see them?" Amy asked Tasha as Eric took off. "And say, did you notice that Jeanine wasn't with the clique?"

"Maybe they kicked her out," Tasha said. "If they did, Jeanine doesn't know how lucky she is."

Amy had to laugh. "Wow, have you changed your tune. Just last week you thought they were so cool."

"Well, I was wrong, and I admit it," Tasha said. "I think they're mean. The way Kyle's been treating Eric—I know Melissa has to be putting him up to that. And the way she talked about Marcy Pringle at the mall! The girl practically choked to death, and all Melissa could think about was her friend getting to sing the solo."

"They're certainly loyal to their friends," Amy

agreed. "When Kelly Marcus broke her leg yesterday, Tracee was actually happy because now her friend Blair will be the head cheerleader."

Tasha was distracted by the sight of a man wheeling a cart full of newspapers into the lobby. "Ooh, there's the *News!*" She hurried over to the corner where the bundles of papers were being dumped and barely gave the man time to cut the twine before grabbing one. Amy took one too and began looking through it.

She saw the usual stuff: sports reports, an editorial about recycling, the gossip column. "Where's the article about the money?"

Tasha didn't reply. She was staring at the front page of the newspaper and was clearly bewildered. "It's not here," she said, pointing. "The article. It was supposed to be the lead story."

The space on the front page that Tasha indicated displayed a grainy photo of Melissa, with the words WEL-COME BACK above it.

"I don't know where this came from," said Tasha. "I saw the copy before it went to the printer's, and this photo wasn't there." She looked up at the clock on the wall. "It's five minutes till the warning bell. I'm going to the *News* office and see if anyone knows what happened."

As Tasha headed up the stairs, Amy went back to reading the newspaper. Before long Eric returned, and now he looked really disturbed.

"What was that all about?" she asked him. "Spence and Kyle?"

He shook his head. "Just Spence." He glanced around at the passing students and lowered his voice to a whisper. "He's disappeared."

"What!"

"He never went home after basketball practice yesterday."

Amy gasped. "Do you think he went looking for Sarah? Or maybe they did run away together!"

"I don't know," Eric said. "This doesn't sound like Spence. He's always been such a sensible person. Not the runaway type. Neither is Sarah."

"Could they both have been kidnapped?" Amy wondered.

"None of the parents have received ransom notes or anything like that. Listen, don't tell anyone about this, okay? I'm not even supposed to be telling you. The principal doesn't want this to get around. Kids could get upset and parents might start freaking out."

"Okay," Amy said. "But I don't see how they can keep something like this a secret."

She was even more convinced of this once she got to homeroom. Just after the roll call, there was a knock on the classroom door. A second later Mrs. Bryant, Jeanine's mother, came in.

"Good morning, Ms. Weller," she chirped. "I got permission to come up because Jeanine forgot her wallet this morning. I brought it here for her." She gazed out over the class, and her bright smile faded.

"But Jeanine isn't here," Ms. Weller said. "I just called roll, and she's absent."

"Absent?" Mrs. Bryant said faintly. "But that's not possible. She left home at her usual time and . . . where could she be?"

"Has anyone seen Jeanine?" Ms. Weller asked the class, but no one had.

Mrs. Bryant's face went white. Hastily Ms. Weller led her out of the room, but the class could hear the woman start to sob in the hallway.

In less than an hour the entire population of Parkside Middle School knew that three students were missing.

And they weren't the only ones. When Amy returned home from school that afternoon, her mother was in a visible state of alarm.

"Amy, what's going on at your school? I just had a call from the president of the PTA. She says there's an epidemic of students running away from home!"

Amy tried to calm her. "Three students don't make an epidemic, Mom. And no one knows for sure that they've run away."

"Then they could have been kidnapped, which is even worse! Amy, has anyone approached you?"

Amy shook her head. There had been times in the past when she'd been approached by strangers, and times when she'd sensed she was being followed and watched. But lately her life had been pretty calm.

"A special PTA meeting has been called for tonight," her mother told her. "I want you to come with me."

Amy groaned. "Oh, Mom, why?"

"Because I'm not leaving you home alone."

Amy was annoyed. One of her favorite TV programs was on that night, and even if she taped it, it would be too late to watch it when they came home. But later, after dinner, as they left the house for school, she had to admit that she was curious to hear what would be said at this meeting. She knew about kids who had run away from home, but three in the same week was pretty bizarre.

Not really knowing Spence or Sarah, she had no idea what could have made them leave home. As for Jeanine, she'd never suspected that her archenemy had reason to take such action. Jeanine lived in a fabulous house where she had her own stereo, TV, and phone. Her parents gave her everything and let her do anything she wanted. Why would she run away? Kidnapping was more likely in her case. After all, Jeanine's parents were very rich.

Whatever had happened to the students, Nancy Candler was nervous. And for once Amy couldn't blame this on her mother's tendency to worry. It soon became clear that a lot of other parents felt the same. The gym was packed with them. It was so crowded by the time Amy and her mother arrived, they had to take seats way in the back.

The PTA president opened the meeting, then turned it over to the principal. Amy almost felt sorry for the dignified woman at the microphone. Poor Dr. Noble was immediately hit with a barrage of questions.

"We want to know what's going on!"

"What are you doing to protect our children?"

"We demand action! What steps are being taken?"

They questions were coming at the principal so fast, she held her hands up and glared at the parents, just as she did when students fooled around and made noise in assemblies.

"Please, please, let me make a statement," she said sternly. "All questions will be answered to the best of our abilities. But nothing can be accomplished if you don't all settle down." Dr. Noble's strong presence and commanding demeanor sent a hush over the crowd.

But what she had to say told them nothing new. She relayed what was known about the disappearances, which wasn't very much, and she assured them that the police were working around the clock. Then she turned the meeting over to the police detective in charge of the investigation, and he talked about the leads they were pursuing, or rather the leads they hoped to establish soon. A psychologist talked about why a child might run away, and a counselor talked about what parents should tell their children.

All in all, no one was saying anything that wasn't

already known. When the audience was invited to ask questions, the same ones were asked over and over again. And the same answers were given.

Besides her ability to hear what others couldn't hear, Amy could also shut out sound if she concentrated hard. She did this and tried to come up with some answers of her own. She started by thinking about any possible connection that might have existed among the three missing students. Spence and Sarah were easy: They were boyfriend and girlfriend. The most obvious answer was that they had run off together. But Eric had said that wasn't possible. Spence was too upset about Sarah's disappearance. So maybe Sarah had been angry at her parents and had run away from home, and Spence had gone looking for her.

But how did Jeanine fit in? As far as Amy knew, Jeanine had no connection with Sarah or Spence. So they must have had friends or acquaintances in common. Parkside Middle School wasn't that big. But what could common friends lead to?

In front of the crowd, someone was going on about tightened security procedures at school and in the neighborhood. Bored and restless, Amy looked around to see if any other kids from school were there. She spotted Linda, Jeanine's former best friend. Linda didn't look too distressed. She was probably still mad about Jeanine's dumping her to hang with Melissa's crowd.

Now, *that* was a connection. Melissa Mitchell . . . they all knew her. And what was even more interesting was the fact that Melissa didn't like any of the three. Could she have something to do with their disappearing?

The assembly did nothing to calm Nancy. Coming out of the gym, she murmured about changing her teaching schedule so that she could drive Amy to school every morning and pick her up every afternoon. Amy had the feeling she wouldn't be allowed out of the house without a bodyguard.

They were just outside the gym entrance and heading to the parking lot when Nancy saw Mr. and Mrs. Morgan, Tasha and Eric's parents. She waved to them, and they stopped to talk. Amy strolled toward her mother's car and waited impatiently. The Morgans lived right next door, for crying out loud. Her mother could talk to them anytime.

"Hello, Amy."

The familiar, disturbing voice came from behind her. Amy turned around and froze. Her breath came out in a rush.

"You . . ."

It was Mr. Devon, the former assistant principal at Parkside, who had displayed an unusual interest in her months earlier. He had left his job as abruptly as he'd appeared, but he kept popping up in Amy's life. Each time she ran into him, he seemed to know more about her. More than she knew about herself.

He stood in the shadows, not smiling but looking calm and relaxed.

Sometimes it seemed as if he was watching out for her. But she was never completely sure about his intentions. The last time she had seen him had been in the hospital in New York City, where he'd seemed to be aligned with the organization that was seeking her. Or had he been trying to rescue her? The answer didn't really matter. It had all been a dream, right?

"What are you doing here?" Amy asked bluntly.

"I heard about this meeting," he said. "Strange, all these disappearances."

"This is none of your business."

He ignored her tone. "What do you know about the clique, Amy?"

"What clique?"

"You know the one."

"I don't belong to any cliques."

"Maybe you should." Mr. Devon unfolded a copy of the *News* that he'd held under his arm. "It could be interesting. You could learn something that might be helpful."

Amy stared at him. What could he be getting at? What did he want from her? She was torn, wanting to know more but not trusting him.

"Amy, who are you talking to?" her mother asked sharply. She reached the car and saw the figure in the shadows. "Oh. It's you. What do you want?"

"I was just talking to Amy about the recent events at school," Mr. Devon said.

Nancy put a protective arm around her daughter. "I don't want Amy getting involved. I'm not going to risk her getting kidnapped too."

"No one's been kidnapped, Ms. Candler."

"How can you be so sure?" Nancy demanded.

"I'm sure," he said simply. "Amy's not in any danger. But others might be." He shifted his focus to Amy. Amy felt her mother's arm tighten around her shoulders.

"Amy is *not* getting involved," Nancy declared firmly. "Come on, honey, let's go home."

A wave of relief passed over Amy as she and Nancy

got into the car and drove away. But a twinge of curiosity forced her to look back at Mr. Devon.

He was watching her, with a knowing look that made her distinctly uncomfortable.

Eric wasn't supposed to step out of the house. Concerned about the disappearances, his parents had ordered him and Tasha to stay home while they were at the PTA meeting. But Tasha had gone to bed early. And Eric wanted to talk to Kyle.

Several times at school that day he'd encountered his former friend. And each time, Kyle had turned away. In fact, Kyle had looked very uncomfortable, as if embarrassed to see Eric. As if he was scared . . . but what of?

And then there were the notes. For the past few days, Eric had found notes stuck into the door of his locker. Strange notes that didn't make any sense. *Mind your own business,* one of them read. *Don't stick your nose in places where it doesn't belong,* read another.

Phone calls, too. The person on the other end hung up when he answered. If Tasha or one of his parents picked up the receiver, the caller asked for Eric—and then hung up when Eric came to the phone.

Kyle wouldn't be doing this. But maybe one of his new friends would.

With any luck, Kyle was home tonight. If his parents had gone to the special PTA meeting, Kyle would be baby-sitting his kid brother. If Eric could just confront him face-to-face, away from the school crowd, maybe he could learn what was up with him. What exactly had changed him.

It was a short walk to the split-level house where Kyle lived. The house appeared to be dark as Eric arrived at the edge of the front yard. But as he walked up the driveway, he saw a dim light shining through closed curtains on the lower level.

He knew Kyle's house well, and he knew that that window was in Kyle's bedroom. He decided not to ring the doorbell and risk waking Kyle's baby brother. He crept along the side of the house until he reached the window, where he could rap for Kyle's attention.

He was about to do just that when he realized Kyle wasn't alone in his room. He heard nothing, but he could make out shadows behind the white curtains. Not just one shadow, or two . . . there had to be at least five people in the room. Maybe Kyle was taking advantage of his parents' absence to have a little party, but there was no music, no loud talking, no television blaring, and no laughter.

As far as Eric could tell, there was nothing but silence. If only he had Amy's super hearing skills . . .

He jumped as the glare of car headlights moved over him. Were Kyle's parents home? Was the PTA meeting over already? If so, he was in trouble.

But the car paused at the foot of the driveway, then moved on. In the flash of light, Eric caught a glimpse of his watch. The meeting would probably be over pretty soon. His own parents would be coming home, and this was no time for him to risk getting grounded.

With one last look at the shadows behind the curtain, he took off for home.

s**6**x

Amy was surprised to hear a knock on the door while she was eating breakfast. It was a good fifteen minutes before Tasha was supposed to be on her doorstep, and Tasha was never early to pick her up for their walk to school. In fact, only in the past year had she begun arriving on time.

But it wasn't Tasha. "Eric!" Amy said as she opened the front door. "What are you doing here so early? Where's Tasha?"

Eric glanced furtively back at his own front door. "I have to talk to you," he said. "In private."

"Okay." Amy was taken aback by the urgency in his tone. "Come on in."

They didn't get any privacy right away. Nancy was coming down the stairs. "Hi, Eric," she said. "I'm glad to see you."

The enthusiasm in her voice clearly surprised him. "You are?" he asked.

"Eric, I'm always pleased to see you."

"Oh, I believe you, Ms. Candler," Eric said agreeably. "But you don't usually *say* it."

"I'm just glad to see you kids together," Nancy said. "I'm very worried about what's going on at your school, and I don't want Amy out alone. I think you should stick together, travel in groups. There's safety in numbers, you know."

Eric grinned. "Yeah, I feel much safer with Amy around. She'll protect me from kidnappers."

Nancy did not appreciate his sense of humor. "Eric, Amy may be stronger than the average twelve-year-old girl—"

"Or fourteen-year-old boy," Eric added.

"But that doesn't mean she isn't susceptible to danger," Nancy continued. "And you know what I mean."

Eric sobered. "Yes, I know. We'll watch out for each other, I promise."

Nancy's expression eased a bit, and she went back to the kitchen. Quickly Eric began to explain his problem to Amy.

"I went to Kyle's last night. The house was dark, so I went to his bedroom window. I couldn't see anything clearly, and I couldn't hear anything, but I swear there were people in the room. It gave me the creeps. I think they were having some sort of secret meeting."

"You mean, like a ceremony?" Amy frowned. "I think you're imagining things. They might be an exclusive clique, but they're not vampires or anything!"

"There's definitely something very weird going on," Eric insisted. "I'm really worried about Kyle. I think he's getting himself into something—I don't know. Something bad."

"He's a big boy, he can take care of himself," said Amy.

Eric shook his head. "I'm not so sure about that. Kyle's a good guy, but he's not very confident. He was never a great athlete, and his grades aren't too hot either. He doesn't have a whole lot of self-esteem, y'know? I think he can be pushed around pretty easily."

"You're his friend," Amy said. "Talk to him."

"I've tried, but he won't even let me get close! Amy . . . you have to help me. You could find out what's going on with that group, what they're having these meetings about."

Amy sank down on the sofa. "Oh, Eric . . . ," she moaned, and wondered if she could make him understand that she just didn't want to get involved. For once in her life, trouble wasn't following *her*. She was living like a normal person, doing normal things and having normal problems. Her mother might be worried about her general safety, but at least she was worrying about the same stuff other parents worried about. And now Eric wanted her to become entangled with *his* problem. She'd already told Mr. Devon she didn't want to get mixed up with this. If only she could make Eric understand . . .

Immediately she felt ashamed. Eric had been there for her many times. It was one thing to tell Mr. Devon she wouldn't help him—she didn't even know if he was on her side. But Eric was someone she could count on. He should be able to count on her.

"Okay," she sighed. "What can I do?"

But there was no time for further discussion. Tasha was in front of the house.

"Don't say anything about this to her," Eric whispered as they went to the door. "That clique is dangerous."

"Oh, come on," Amy said. "They're just kids like us, only snottier."

Eric shook his head. "I'm not so sure about that. Let's just leave Tasha out of it."

Tasha was startled to see her brother at Amy's, but she wasn't particularly suspicious. "What have you two been up to?" she asked with a wise look.

Amy replied in the same fashion. "Wouldn't you like to know?"

On the way to school they tried to avoid the topic of Kyle, Melissa, and the clique, but everything seemed to come back to that. Tasha was still speculating on the mystery about the *News* article.

"Nobody can figure out what happened," she told them. "Everything was on a floppy disk, including the article about the money. Somehow, when the newspaper was printed, the article had been replaced by that photo of Melissa. It doesn't make any sense."

"Could someone have deleted the article from the disk and scanned in the photo?" Eric wondered.

"Not possible," Tasha said. "The disk was never out of our hands. The editor herself delivered it to the printer."

"Well, obviously a friend of Melissa's did it," Amy said. "Is she tight with someone on the newspaper staff?"

"Well, yeah," Tasha admitted. "Blair Cavanaugh writes the stupid gossip column."

"So she must have switched the copy!" Amy declared.

Tasha shook her head. "She never had her hands on the disk. In fact, she was late with her article, so she had to drop it off separately at the printer's."

Amy still thought that Blair had to be responsible. But Tasha insisted that once the disk had been delivered to the printer, no one else could touch it. And it was very unlikely that Melissa had any special friends who worked at the printing shop.

Still, it was interesting, Amy thought as she gazed at the clique's table at lunchtime in the cafeteria, that everything that was happening seemed to have some sort of connection to them. The disappearances were connected to Melissa. When Kelly broke her leg, Blair became head cheerleader. Kristy profited from Marcy's choking on a mushroom. But it wasn't as if Blair had broken Kelly's leg, and Kristy hadn't shoved the mushroom down Marcy's throat. Amy supposed it could all be coincidence . . . but there were just too many coincidences for her to accept that.

Tasha's voice broke into her thoughts. "Why are you staring at *them*?"

Amy rearranged her features to appear more nonchalant. "Oh, no reason. Just thinking about how exclusive they are."

"And evil," Tasha said.

"That's pretty harsh."

"Well, haven't you noticed how they have something to do with all the weird things that have been happening at school?"

"Don't be silly," Amy said quickly. "It's just a bunch of coincidences."

She wished she could really believe that. And when she went to her French class that afternoon, she was particularly friendly to Tracee, her one real contact with the clique. If Amy was going to help Eric help Kyle, she had to get closer to the group and figure out what they were all about.

Tracee was carrying a copy of the *News*. "Did you see the photo of Melissa?" she asked Amy. "Isn't that awesome? No one's ever had a photo that large in the *News*."

"Yes, it's a nice picture," Amy agreed. "It was very thoughtful of the editor to put it in the paper."

"The editor?" Tracee said with a sneer. "Do you know, when we asked her to put Melissa's photo in the paper, she said there wasn't any space? She's just jealous, because Melissa is so pretty and she's such a dog."

"Then how did the picture get in the paper?"

"Oh, well, it turned out that some space was available after all," Tracee said, becoming vague. She changed the subject. "We're not having a pop quiz today, are we?"

"Not a regular quiz," Amy replied. "But remember, Madame Duquesne said she was going to grade us on our oral responses today."

"Oh, no," Tracee moaned. "And the warning notices go out next week! If my parents see that I'm failing this class again, I'm going to be grounded for life."

Amy saw a chance to get closer to Tracee. "Listen, I could help you in French, if you want," she offered.

"Can I copy off your paper?" Tracee asked eagerly.

Amy shifted uncomfortably in her seat. "It's an *oral* quiz, Tracee. But look, if you don't do well today, we can tell Madame Duquesne that I'm going to work with you after school, and maybe she won't be so hard on you in the warning notice."

Tracee smiled. "That's not necessary. I know an easier way."

"You do?" Amy grimaced. "I hope you're not thinking of breaking into the school's computer system. My boyfriend told me that someone tried to change their grade that way last year, and ended up suspended."

Tracee laughed. "Are you kidding? I don't even know how to turn on a computer!"

The bell rang, and Madame Duquesne walked in. *"Bonjour, mes élèves,"* she said, and the class responded with the usual *"Bonjour, Madame."* Then the teacher went right into the oral quiz.

She walked around the class, asking each student a question in French, such as "What time is it?" or "What did you eat for breakfast?" Amy was trying to figure out how to say "cornflakes" in French when she noticed that Tracee was watching the teacher intently, following Madame Duquesne closely with her eyes as she moved up and down the aisles.

As the teacher drew closer to their desks, Amy realized that Tracee was actually looking just over the teacher's head. Amy looked up too and saw that Tracee had her eyes fixed on a light fixture. A light fixture that seemed to be loose . . .

"Madame!" Amy cried. "Watch out!"

But Madame wasn't fast enough. The light fixture fell from the ceiling and gave her a glancing blow on the side of the head. She collapsed on the floor.

The room erupted in chaos. "Get water!" someone screamed, while someone else yelled, "I'll go for the principal," and raced out of the room.

Amy knelt by the teacher's side. Madame Duquesne was very still, but Amy could feel a pulse in her wrist. "Don't touch her," she told the others who had gathered around. "We have to wait for help."

She'd almost forgotten about Tracee until she rose

and found the girl standing next to her. Tracee didn't appear the least bit upset.

"I've heard of being saved by the bell," she joked. "But this is the first time I've been saved by a light!"

Aghast, Amy stared at her. Then she remembered her mission and forced herself to smile.

"Yeah. Cool."

se7en

It hadn't been easy, pretending to laugh along with Tracee over Madame Duquesne's accident. But it paid off. When Amy ran into Tracee near her locker after the last period, Tracee was friendlier than usual.

"I just saw someone who works in the principal's office," she confided to Amy. "Madame Duquesne is going to be in the hospital at least three weeks!"

"Was she badly hurt?" Amy asked.

Tracee shrugged. "Don't know. But I *do* know that she won't be sending out any warning notices next week!"

Amy faked a look of relief. "That's great news. Congratulations!"

"And when you told me about the person who tried to break into the computer system, that gave me an idea," Tracee continued. "I think I can arrange things so I won't have to worry about any of my grades."

"I thought you said you don't know anything about computers," Amy said, trying to hide her alarm.

"I don't. But I'm going to talk to Melissa about it."

"Melissa? Is she a computer whiz?"

"No. Not exactly. Hey, what are you doing now?"

"Just going home," Amy said.

"Want to come to the mall with me and Kristy? Her sister's picking us up here and dropping us off."

Amy was pleased. There was something about shopping at the mall that brought girls closer together. This was a perfect opportunity to get a foot into the clique. She wouldn't even have to make up an explanation to give Tasha, who had gymnastics after school today. They wouldn't have been walking home together anyway.

Kristy didn't look quite so pleased when Tracee showed up with Amy. "You're a friend of Tasha Morgan's," she said accusingly.

Amy recalled the incident on the school steps when Tasha had said that Marcy was the best singer in the chorus. She remembered Tracee's telling her that Kristy hated Tasha.

"We're not really friends," Amy lied. "She lives next door to me, so our mothers make us do things together."

Kristy looked at her skeptically. "You shouldn't let your mother push you around. Just tell her you're old enough to choose your own friends."

"Thanks for the advice," Amy said. "I'll do that."

A car pulled up, driven by a teenage girl who was as pretty as Kristy. The girls piled in, and Kristy continued talking on the way to the mall.

"You're only in the seventh grade, right?" she asked Amy.

Amy had to admit that was true.

"It must be tough for you," Tracee said.

"Isn't ninth grade a lot harder than seventh grade?" Amy asked.

Kristy and Tracee laughed. "That's not what she means," Kristy told Amy. "She means it's *socially* tough."

"Because there are so many nerds in the seventh

grade," Tracee explained. "And I know that for a fact from French class. What a bunch of losers! Except you, of course," she added hastily.

Kristy didn't appear quite so ready to consider Amy an exception to the rule. "We've got plenty of low-life dorks in ninth grade too, but most seventh-graders are totally clueless." She turned to Tracee. "Like the last seventh-grader who tried to hang out with us."

Tracee made a face. "Do you know Jeanine Bryant?" she asked Amy.

For once that day, Amy didn't have to fake anything. She had no problem making a face as strong as Tracee's. "I can't stand Jeanine Bryant. We've been enemies since first grade."

That comment scored her points with Kristy. "She does think she's hot stuff," Kristy agreed. "And we thought she was okay at first. But then Melissa came back to school, and she made us realize how Jeanine was trying to worm her way into our group. She really got on Melissa's nerves."

Amy got up some nerve of her own. "I wonder where Jeanine is now," she said casually.

"Who knows?" Kristy said, and it seemed to Amy that she really didn't know. Or care.

Sunshine Square was full of the usual after-school crowds. Sometimes Amy wondered how the sales-people felt about the students who descended upon them every day. Most students just hung around, window shopping, and tried on clothes they couldn't afford to buy. This clique seemed to be no different. Amy followed Kristy and Tracee to a record store, where they listened to a bunch of new CDs but didn't make a purchase. Then they hit the boutiques and the shoe stores. Tracee moaned over a pair of mock-alligator ankle boots that fit her perfectly, but she didn't buy them. At a cosmetics counter, Kristy tried a lipstick that looked great on her. Even the saleswoman commented on it.

"That's a gorgeous color for your skin tone," she told Kristy. "And it's on sale, only three ninety-nine."

Kristy admired herself in the mirror. "I love it," she said, but even though the lipstick wasn't expensive, she didn't buy it.

All the while, Amy searched for an opportunity to bring up the subject of Melissa and Kyle. She knew she had to be careful. Tracee liked her, but Kristy was still giving her suspicious looks, obviously trying to figure out what right Amy had to be with them. So Amy kept her mouth shut for the time being and acted like she enjoyed window shopping.

Her chance came just after they left the cosmetics store. Kristy looked at her watch. "It's time to meet Melissa," she announced.

"Oh, is Melissa coming to the mall?" Amy asked, hoping her interest sounded appropriately casual.

Tracee nodded. "She has her regular doctor's appointment in the medical building here. We're supposed to meet her in the food court, at Taco Pronto."

Melissa was already there, waiting alone at a table. She smiled and waved when she saw Kristy and Tracee, but her smile disappeared when she realized Amy was with them.

"What's *she* doing here?" she demanded of her friends.

Amy was a little surprised by her attitude. Melissa didn't have any reason to dislike her. Or so she thought.

"Amy's in my French class," Tracee told her. "She's okay, really."

Melissa's eyes were cold. "She's Eric Morgan's girlfriend."

There was no way Amy could deny that. Melissa had

seen her with Eric, and no doubt Kyle had described their relationship.

"Why are you mad at Eric?" Amy asked.

"Because he's bugging Kyle." Melissa frowned. "He keeps calling him at home and trying to talk to him at school. He wants Kyle to feel bad about being with me. He wants to break us up."

"That's not true," Amy told her. "He's just unhappy because Kyle isn't hanging out with him anymore."

"Kyle's old friends are a bunch of nerds," Melissa said flatly. "He's becoming cool now. And I want Eric to leave him alone." After a moment she added, "Or else."

Or else what? Amy wanted to ask. But something about Melissa's expression told her she shouldn't. "I'll talk to Eric," she said humbly. "You know, I was telling him just the other day that Kyle has the right to make his own decisions."

"You said that to Eric?" Melissa asked doubtfully.

Amy nodded. "It's not that Eric means to be nosy. He cares about people. He worries about me all the time."

"Why?" Kristy asked.

Amy hesitated. What would impress this group and make them accept her?

"Well, I'm very independent. I don't like anyone telling me what to do, not even Eric. He doesn't like me to have secrets from him."

"And do you have secrets?" Melissa asked with interest.

Amy could honestly answer yes to that. But she played it safe. "Let's just say I don't think I have to tell everyone everything about me," she answered.

The girls from the clique looked at each other and smiled. "That's how we feel," Melissa said. "That's why I don't like it when Eric bugs Kyle. It's like he's trying to find out stuff he's got no business knowing."

"Sometimes Eric can be very uncool," Amy murmured. "You know how boys are."

Melissa turned to Tracee. "Speaking of boys, have you made any progress with Jay?"

"No," Tracee said mournfully. "I think maybe he likes Dorie Flanders."

"Well, we can take care of that," Melissa said comfortingly.

Amy had no idea who or what they were talking about, but recalling Melissa's dislike of busybodies, she didn't ask any questions. Instead she expressed concern for Melissa. "How are you feeling?" she asked. "Tracee said you had a doctor's appointment today."

"Oh, I'm fine," Melissa assured her. "I don't even go to the appointments anymore. I just let my mother drop me off at the medical building and I go shopping in the mall."

"Talk about shopping," Kristy said, "wait till you see what I got today." She reached into her purse and pulled out two CDs.

"Ooh, I'm dying to hear that!" Melissa cried.

Amy was stunned. She hadn't noticed Kristy buying anything in the record store.

"Check this out," Tracee said. She opened her shoulder bag and brought out the alligator boots she'd tried on. Then Kristy showed off her new lipstick.

Amy stifled a gasp. It was clear to her now that all these items had been shoplifted. But how? She'd been with Kristy and Tracee the whole time, and surely she would have noticed something. Maybe not something small like a lipstick, but a pair of boots?

And when Kristy dug into her bag again, she brought out a big fat stuffed animal. Amy was completely bewildered. There was no way Kristy could have shoved that toy into her bag without anyone's seeing her.

"Isn't he cute?" Kristy crooned.

"Adorable," Melissa agreed. She turned to Amy. "Pretty good haul, huh?"

Amy swallowed. "Amazing. You guys are really good at this."

Melissa smiled. "Well, we have our secrets too."

eight

Tasha was bewildered. "Why do you have to eat lunch with her every day?"

Amy had expected this question. She'd been prepared ever since she'd been invited to join the members of the clique at their lunch table the day before.

"Well, like I said, Tracee wants me to tutor her in French. She's actually paying me for it!" Amy said smoothly. "And she wants me to sit with her at lunch so we can practice speaking French."

"But you've been sitting with the whole clique! How can you be giving lessons to Tracee with all those other girls around?"

"It's not easy," Amy assured her. "But Tracee just refuses to be separated from her friends."

Tasha spoke stiffly. "It's nice that *some* people still feel that way about their friends."

She was hurt, that was clear. But what could Amy do? She looked at Eric, hoping for some help, but Eric was walking ahead of them in the hall, pretending not to hear the conversation. What a coward, Amy thought bitterly. But she was sworn to secrecy, and there was no way she could even hint to Tasha the real reason for her new lunch mates.

This would be her third day eating lunch with the clique. And what was she getting from the experience? Absolutely nothing—just a lot of chatter and gossip and complaints about all the nerds, dorks, and assorted clueless wimps who made life at Parkside Middle School miserable for the cool people. Not that the so-called nerds actually did anything to the popular kids— it was their mere existence that made the world less pleasant. Amy just kept on agreeing, complimenting Melissa and the others on their assessment of people and adding an occasional spiteful remark of her own.

But she'd learned nothing about Kyle. Melissa mentioned him occasionally, but Amy hadn't spoken to him at all, obeying the unwritten rule about sex segregation in the cafeteria. Nothing had been said about the people who had disappeared, either. Or the head cheerleader, who had broken her leg, or Marcy, who had choked on a mushroom . . . Amy was beginning to wonder if maybe all those strange events really were coincidental.

She knew one thing for sure. She wasn't going to continue this game indefinitely. No matter how much Eric cared about Kyle, nothing was worth hurting Tasha over. Amy saw that her friend was biting her lower lip to keep it from trembling, and she vowed to herself that if nothing interesting happened in the cafeteria this afternoon, the game would end very soon.

At lunchtime Amy carried her tray from the cafeteria line to the table where Melissa was holding court. The girls were unusually quiet as she approached, and Amy felt her stomach jump. Had they figured out she was spying on them? And what if they had? It wasn't like any of them could do anything to her. With her superior physical strength, Amy could take them all on with very little effort.

But the five girls sitting at the table didn't seem to be

up for a fight. Four of them were looking at Melissa. And Melissa was smiling.

"Hi, guys," Amy said lightly as she put down her tray. Unfortunately, Tasha passed right in front of them at that very moment. She saw Amy, but she didn't speak. In fact, she made a big show of tossing her head and looking the other way. Amy's insides ached at how much her best friend was hurting, and she almost called out to her.

But before she could, Kristy spoke. "You've actually dumped that toad, huh?" she asked, and Amy could hear the satisfaction in her voice.

Amy clenched her fists under the table but forced a grin. "Yeah. She was a royal pain."

The girls looked at each other, then at Amy. She could read the approval in their faces. Melissa took over.

"Amy, I was wondering if you'd like to come over to my place tonight. My parents are going out, so we're going to have a little . . . well, a party, sort of."

Amy was suddenly aware that her heart was beating just a little faster. She tried not to let her excitement show. "Sure, I'd love to," she said nonchalantly. "Should I bring anything? Potato chips? CDs? I've got some good dance music."

Blair Cavanaugh started giggling, but Melissa shot her a look that shut her up fast. "No, you don't need to bring anything," she said. "We won't be dancing. And Amy . . ." She paused. "Don't bring Eric. I know he's your boyfriend, but I just don't think he'd fit in."

"No problem," Amy said. She glanced across the cafeteria to where Eric was sitting with his friends. There was no way she could get up to let him know about her invitation. But later she would alert him that new information might be coming very soon. "A party, sort of," Melissa had said. That had to mean one of their secret meetings.

Only "later" didn't come for Amy and Eric. They didn't have any classes near each other, and he went directly to the gym for basketball practice after school. Amy was on her own.

What does a person wear to a sort-of-party secret meeting? Amy wondered as she looked through her closet early that evening. Her mother appeared at her bedroom door.

"Are Tasha and Eric going to this party with you?" she asked.

"No," Amy told her. "It's a different crowd."

Nancy picked up a T-shirt Amy had left on the floor and began folding it. "Oh, these are new friends?" Her tone was carefully casual, but Amy caught the undercurrent of concern. She tried to keep her response equally casual.

"Yeah, kind of. One of the girls is in my French class, and she introduced me to the others." She turned to her mother. "Don't worry, Mom. I'm not going to tell them any secrets about myself."

The relief on her mother's face was unmistakable. "Good. I can deal with the fact that Tasha and Eric know all about you. But the fewer people who do, the better."

What would this new crowd think if they found out I'm a clone? Amy wondered. Would it raise her higher in their esteem? Or put her in the category of nerd? She would never know their reaction because they weren't going to find out. She wasn't going to let her secret become the talk of Blair Cavanaugh's gossip column, or even the talk of the clique. They spent way too much time dishing people for Amy to trust them with a secret that big. She had to concentrate on learning *their* secrets.

Melissa's home wasn't anything special, just a typical

California ranch-style house. Nancy pulled into the empty driveway to let Amy off. "Have a good time," she said. "And call me if you can't get a ride home." Then, looking ahead at the closed carport doors, she asked, "This girl's parents are home, aren't they?"

Amy managed a noncommittal "Mmmm" and got out of the car before her mother could ask any more questions.

For a house in which a party was supposed to be taking place, it seemed awfully quiet, and for a moment Amy wondered if she had the right address. But the door opened less than a second after she knocked. Kyle stood there.

Amy turned to wave to her mother. When she looked back at Kyle, he had a suprised look on his face. Apparently Melissa had not told him Amy was coming.

"What are you doing here?" he blurted out.

"I was invited," she said. "Can I come in?"

He stepped aside and looked beyond her. "Is Eric coming too?" he asked nervously. "Does he know about this?"

"No to both questions," Amy replied. She brushed past him and went into a dimly lit living room.

If she had expected something that looked like a cult

or a séance group, she would have been disappointed. There were no candles burning, no New Age music floating through the room. People were standing or sprawled on the furniture, and it really did look like a meeting. As far as appearances went, they could have been the committee that was planning the homecoming float.

Melissa was clearly the committee chairperson. "Hi, Amy, come on in. Do you know everyone?" She led Amy around the room and introduced her. Amy knew Tracee, of course, and Kristy and Blair, and she'd met Lori Kessler, the ninth-grade treasurer. Of the boys she knew only Kyle, who was still looking very apprehensive. The other two, Jeff and Dean, were guys she vaguely recognized from school.

Jeff didn't seem too pleased to see her. "She's a seventh-grader!" he declared. "Why do we want *her* around?"

Tracee stood up for her. "Because she's cool. You should have seen Amy's face when the lighting fixture fell on Madame Duquesne! She loved it. And you liked the way I made the tests disappear, didn't you, Amy?"

Amy was disconcerted. "You made the tests disappear?"

"You're going too fast," Melissa scolded Tracee. "Amy, just have a seat and listen. You'll catch on."

Once everyone was settled Melissa became business-like. "Now, we don't have too much time—my parents will be back in an hour. First of all, Kyle, how's your practice coming along? Are you going to be ready for the game next week?"

Kyle nodded. "I'm ready now. I've been practicing a lot."

Amy was surprised to hear this. Eric had told her Kyle had completely stopped showing up for basketball sessions.

"You don't want to look too obvious," Dean warned him. "Don't make the ball turn a hundred and eighty degrees in midair. Try to throw it in the general direction of the basket, okay? Otherwise people are going to wonder."

"I'll do the best I can," Kyle said stiffly.

"Don't nag Kyle," Melissa said to Dean. "If it wasn't for him, I wouldn't be here, remember?"

"Oh, come on, don't exaggerate," Dean said. "You could have sent that car off into outer space before it came close to you."

"That's true," Melissa admitted. "But I didn't know that then, did I?"

Amy looked at her in utter puzzlement. What were

they talking about? How could Melissa send a car into outer space? But she kept her mouth shut. She had a feeling all would be revealed eventually.

Melissa beamed at Kyle. "If you can pull this off, you could become a basketball star, you know. You won't even have to finish high school. Every team will want you. You can be rich and famous, bigger than Michael Jordan!"

Kyle smiled thinly. The prospect didn't seem to be giving him a thrill.

"The next item on the agenda," Melissa said, "is Dorie Flanders. Kristy thinks Jay Dillard is interested in her, and she wants to send her away. Any discussion?"

Kristy spoke up. "Actually, I might be wrong about that. Jay asked me out for tomorrow night."

Melissa nodded. "All right, we'll table the question of Dorie. Is there any old business we need to discuss?"

"What about Eric Morgan?" Jeff asked. "The guy's getting to be a pain."

Amy had been trying to keep her face impassive, but the mention of Eric's name made her let out an inadvertent gasp. Melissa looked at her.

"Do you have something to say, Amy?"

"I—I'm not sure. . . . What's Eric doing?"

"He's still calling me," Kyle said miserably. "He knows something's going on. And . . . and . . . I can't help it, I feel crummy about him. The way he looks at me . . . it's hurting my concentration."

"We've tried to make him nervous," Jeff said. "Prank phone calls, notes in his locker, that sort of thing. But he's not making the connection. I don't think the guy's too bright."

"That's not true!" Amy exclaimed. "Eric is very intelligent! How is he supposed to know what those phone calls and notes mean?"

"I say we should just send him away," Dean declared.

"No!" Kyle cried out. "Don't hurt Eric!"

"No one's talking about hurting anyone," Dean told him. "We would just make him disappear for a while. Like Spence and Sarah. And that obnoxious seventh-grader, what was her name?"

"Jeanine," Blair said.

Kyle was still shaking his head vigorously. "I don't want Eric sent away."

"Okay, I know he was your friend," Melissa said gently. "We won't do anything to him. But if you're going to be really and truly a part of this, you have to lose him." She shifted her attention to Amy. "The same goes for you. Can you handle that? Will you dump Eric?"

Amy didn't know what to say. She looked at Tracee.

Tracee grinned and turned to their leader. "I think she's a little confused, Melissa."

"That's an understatement," Amy answered truthfully.

Melissa nodded. "Okay, I'll try to explain what we're all about. You see, Amy, we can do things."

"Things," Amy repeated. "Like what?"

"We can make a basketball go into a net. We can make tests go away. We can erase floppy disks."

Kristy spoke. "Remember at school when Tasha tripped on the front steps, and when she tripped again in the cafeteria? I made that happen."

"Did you hear about Kelly Marcus breaking her leg?" Blair asked.

"You broke Kelly's leg?" Amy asked.

Blair grinned. "Not exactly. I just made her land badly from a jump. Melissa taught me how to do that."

"And I can teach you, too, Amy," Melissa said. "If you join us. Now, I know what you're thinking."

"You can read minds too?" Amy asked faintly.

Melissa laughed. "No, I mean I can guess what

you're wondering about. You want to know who taught *me*, right? Well, no one did. It was a little something I picked up in the hospital."

Amy listened to the story in wonderment. It turned out that while Melissa was being treated for the head injuries she'd suffered in the car accident, the doctors had used experimental radioactive ions to prevent brain damage. But the radiation had produced an unexpected result.

"I can move things with my mind," Melissa said. "I didn't know this right away, of course. It was that first day back at school, when I was crossing the street and the car almost hit me. I was so mad at that driver, I must have been thinking about what I wanted to happen to him. And then it happened!"

"You made the car turn and hit a tree," Amy recalled.

"That's right! Then at the last basketball game, I really wanted Kyle to get a basket. I thought about it really hard, and I made the ball go into the net!"

"Ohmigod," Amy breathed. Then, to make sure Melissa took this as a compliment, she added, "Awesome."

Melissa went on. "I helped Kristy get the solo part in

the chorus. I didn't plan it; it was a coincidence that Marcy was in the pizza place at the same time I was there. I just made a mushroom stop moving down her throat when she was swallowing. That's why she choked."

Tracee piped up. "We were all so excited when we realized what Melissa could do. And we started begging her to take care of our problems. Like, Blair wanted to be head cheerleader, and I wanted some French tests to disappear."

"But I couldn't be everywhere for everyone," Melissa continued. "And it's not like I can just blink and make things happen. It takes a *lot* of concentration. Anyway, I tried to show Tracee how I made my mind move things—and she was able to pick it up from me! Isn't that amazing?"

"Of course, I'm not as good as Melissa," Tracee said modestly. "None of us are. We can't be too far away from Melissa when we want to make something move, or it won't work at all. But I made the lighting fixture fall on Madame Duquesne. Pretty cool, huh?"

"Cool," Amy echoed. "And you can move people, too, huh?"

"No, that's too hard," Tracee said. "Melissa's the only one who can do that."

"It's not easy for me either," Melissa admitted. "It was really hard when I moved Sarah. She must have a strong personality. Spence was easier, since he was so worried about Sarah. I guess he had so much on his mind, he was weak and couldn't resist the force of my mind." For a moment she seemed sad. "You know, if he'd been just a little more worried about *me* instead of her, he'd be here with us today."

"What about Jeanine?" Amy asked.

"Oh, she was easy. That girl doesn't have much character."

"Where are they all now?"

"I haven't got a clue," Melissa told her. "I just pushed them away. People are harder than things. I can't control where they end up."

"That's our big issue," Kristy said. "Controlling the power and channeling it. We want to see if we can pool our energies and do something really big."

"Something that would make the world a better place," Blair added. "Or at least make Parkside Middle School a lot hipper."

Amy's head was spinning. They all sounded so matter-of-fact, as if they were discussing a canned food drive or gathering blankets for homeless shelters.

"What do you think, Amy?" Tracee asked. "Want to be part of the clique?"

"I was just wondering," Amy said. "Why me? I mean, how come you're asking me to join the group? Do you really think I'm . . . *cool* enough?"

"It's more than that," Melissa said. "Tracee told us that you run amazingly fast. And that you've got super eyesight." She leaned over and looked at Amy keenly. "What other special talents do you have?"

Amy thought. "Well, I also have excellent hearing."

"Is that all?" Dean asked, disappointed. "I thought maybe you had some super-powers."

Amy forced a laugh. "Don't be silly. What do I look like, Wonder Woman?"

"So what's your answer?" Melissa asked. "Will you help us out tomorrow?"

"Tomorrow?"

Melissa lightly slapped the side of her own head. "Oh, am I out of it or *what*? We haven't even told you about the big trial run tomorrow. We're going to try pooling our energies for the first time. Blair, do you have an invitation left that you can show her?"

Blair dug in her bag and took out a flyer, which she handed to Amy. Amy unfolded it and read the message inside.

Greetings and congratulations! You have been selected as one of the outstanding students at Parkside Middle School. A special photo-graph will be taken for the school yearbook.

The notice went on to give the next day's date, a time (one in the afternoon), and a place (the school gym).

"We sent these notices to twenty people we don't like," Blair told her. "Just a general range of nerds in all grades."

"When they arrive at the gym, they'll be arranged together for a photo," Kristy continued. "Jeff's on the yearbook staff, so it will look official. The rest of us will be hiding behind the bleachers."

Melissa took over. "Then, at my signal, we'll all concentrate on sending them away!"

"If it works," Tracee said dreamily, "just think what we could do! We could wipe out the entire nerd population of Parkside Middle School!"

"And of all the middle schools in all the world!" Blair added.

Amy looked at Kyle. He hadn't said a word for a while, and it didn't look like he was going to say anything now. His hands were folded on his lap and his head was bowed in shame. At least Amy hoped that was what he was feeling.

"Well, Amy, what do you think?" Melissa asked brightly. "Pretty cool, huh?"

Amy tore her eyes away from Kyle and looked directly at Melissa.

"Yeah. Cool."

n**i**ne

Coming home from basketball practice, Eric was beat. It had been a crummy session. Since Spence's disappearance, all the energy seemed to have gone out of the team. The guy who had taken over as captain didn't have much spirit, and the coach was in a foul mood. There was a game next week, and no one was up for it.

Normally after a practice session, Eric hung out with Kyle. They talked and joked and horsed around. They complained about Coach, and Eric ended up feeling better. But Kyle wasn't around. He wasn't returning Eric's calls, and he avoided Eric at school.

On top of all that, Eric had found another stupid note in his locker. This one read *Keep a low profile or you won't have any profile at all*. What was that supposed to mean? He couldn't help thinking that this had something to do with Kyle. But Kyle wouldn't do anything so silly. The clique, on the other hand . . . But why would they care? Nothing made any sense to him.

He wanted to talk to someone. Before going to his own house, he stopped next door at Amy's and rang the bell.

Nancy came to the door. "Hi, Eric. Amy's not home."

"Where is she?"

"Visiting a friend."

"What friend?" Then he realized how he must have sounded, and he blushed.

Nancy smiled. "It's a girlfriend, Eric."

"Oh. Okay." He thrust his hands into his pockets and ambled over to his own front door. Who could Amy be visiting? Then he brightened. Maybe she was out picking up some solid information about the clique and Kyle. He just hoped she was being careful.

When Amy woke up on Saturday morning, for one brief, shining moment she thought the events of the night before had been just another one of her weird dreams. But as the reality of the day descended upon her, she knew that it had really happened.

It was hard to take in. She used to think the worst thing a clique could do would be to influence others to change their behavior. Like Kyle. But this clique, this snotty, exclusive group, had somehow managed to develop a power way beyond that.

She had to do something. Something to stop them. But even with her superior skills and physical strength, she couldn't make objects move. Or people.

"Amy! Breakfast!"

Maybe food would make her think better. She got out of bed, threw on a robe, and went downstairs.

"Did you have fun at the party last night?" Nancy asked her as she served French toast.

It was Amy's favorite breakfast, but she wasn't sure she had the appetite to eat it. "Yeah, it was okay."

"Eric came by looking for you."

Amy paused, her fork halfway to her mouth. "Did you tell him where I went?"

"No. Just that you were with a friend. Why?"

"No reason." She shoved the French toast into her mouth and chewed slowly. She had to see Eric today, and she knew that what she'd discovered would only make him worried that he'd gotten her involved. He'd be furious at the clique, too. And Amy didn't want him doing anything rash. The clique was all too ready to send Eric to—to wherever the people they sent away ended up.

"Do you have any plans for today?" Nancy asked, interrupting Amy's thoughts.

"Uh, Melissa's coming over," Amy said.

"Melissa?"

"The girl who had the party last night."

"Oh, of course. What time will she be here?"

"Around eleven."

"Then I'll miss her. Too bad," Nancy said. "I've got that dentist appointment. Maybe she'll still be here when I get back. I like to meet your friends."

Not this one, Amy thought. "Well, we're going to— to this thing, this event, at school around one."

"What kind of event?"

"Something for the yearbook."

Nancy had finished her breakfast. "Okay, well, you have fun. I think I'll go take a shower." She left the table and went upstairs. Amy sat alone. It was almost ten. She had only an hour before Melissa came by. To teach

Amy how to share her power. And then they'd be going over to the school, where twenty unsuspecting students would be waiting to have their photo taken. Twenty boys and girls who would end up . . . who knew where?

Maybe Amy could learn the skill so well that she could keep them here when the others tried to send them away. But Melissa was the one with the real power. Melissa was the key to the situation. The others just fed off her. It was Melissa she had to deal with, Melissa alone. But there was so much Amy didn't know: the extent of Melissa's abilities, her motives, her feelings, her ultimate goals.

Amy knew where to start. Pushing aside her mostly uneaten breakfast, she found the Parkside Middle School student directory and went to the phone.

She did learn one thing about Melissa: The girl was prompt. At precisely eleven o'clock, Melissa rang Amy's doorbell.

"Hi, come in," Amy told her.

Melissa entered the living room and looked around tentatively. "Your mother's not here?"

"No, like I told you last night, she had a dentist appointment."

Melissa wrinkled her nose. "I hate going to the dentist," she said. "I'm supposed to go for a checkup next week." She smiled. "Maybe I should just send the dentist away."

"Ha, ha," Amy said, and hoped she looked sincerely amused. "Are you hungry? Want something to eat?"

"Okay," Melissa said. Amy led her into the kitchen. While Melissa sat down at the kitchen table, Amy perused the contents of the refrigerator.

"Let's see . . . there's half of a chicken, and tomatoes . . . how about a sandwich?"

"Sounds good," Melissa said. "But don't take them out of the refrigerator."

"Huh?"

"Watch this."

Amy got her first real glimpse of Melissa's talent in action. Before her eyes, the platter containing the chicken rose from the shelf, floated out of the refrigerator, and landed on the counter. The vegetable bin opened and two ripe tomatoes jumped out. A head of lettuce and a loaf of bread followed. Finally a jar of mayonnaise edged its way off a shelf and started toward the counter.

The mayonnaise didn't make it, though. Halfway to the counter, it plummeted to the floor.

Melissa gazed in dismay at the shards of glass and gooey white gunk on the tiles. "Sorry about that," she apologized. "Sometimes I miss. I shouldn't be showing off like this for you anyway. It takes a lot of concentration, and my power can weaken. I tell all my crowd not to use their skill for silly reasons. We have to save it for what counts."

Amy nodded. "That's why nobody did anything last night."

"Right," Melissa said. "And I wouldn't be showing you anything now, except . . ."

"Except what?"

"Well, I'm still not absolutely positive about you, Amy. I want to make sure you're really on our side."

Amy swallowed. "What do you want me to do?"

"It's more what we *don't* what you to do," Melissa said. "You can't help us send the nerds away today."

"But I want to help," Amy said. "I told you last night, I want to be just like you guys."

"We just can't trust you yet," Melissa said. "I can't give you the power until I know for sure that you deserve it. You can come with me to school and watch, but that's all for today."

Amy pretended to pout, and then she sighed. "Okay, I

understand." But her brain was working overtime. This was an unexpected blow, and it put an end to one possible resolution she'd considered. Now she wouldn't be able to use Melissa's power against her.

The doorbell rang. Melissa wasn't pleased. "Are you expecting anyone?" she asked.

"No." She went back into the living room, and Melissa followed her. Through the window Amy made out the figure standing on the doorstep. "It's Eric."

To her surprise, Melissa said, "Perfect!"

"Why is that perfect?"

"This gives you a chance to show me your real loyalty. I want to see you get rid of him."

"But . . . But he's still my boyfriend, Melissa. I can't break up with him right this minute!"

"Just lose him for now," Melissa said impatiently. "Today the clique comes first."

"He'll wonder why you're here," Amy pointed out.

"He won't know I'm here," Melissa assured her. "I'll be behind the door." She smiled. "He won't see me, but I'll be able to hear everything you say. You don't mind if I do that, do you? I mean, it's not like you're going to tell him anything I shouldn't hear, right?"

"Of course not," Amy said.

The doorbell rang again. Melissa stood by the door so that when Amy opened it, she wasn't visible.

"Hi," Eric said.

"Hi," Amy echoed.

"Can I come in?"

"Well, actually, this isn't a good time."

"Oh." He looked puzzled and a little hurt. She wished she could give him some sort of signal, a wink or a sign, but she didn't dare.

"I was just wondering if you want to do something this afternoon," he said.

"I've got plans," she said. "Something I have to do. School stuff."

"Are you getting your picture taken too?"

She looked at him blankly. "Huh?"

"I thought maybe you were chosen to be one of those outstanding students. Like Tasha."

"Like Tasha," she repeated dumbly.

"Yeah, she got some flyer about it and has to go to the gym this afternoon to have her picture taken." Eric smirked. "Hope it doesn't go to her head. Well, I'll call you tonight."

"Yes," Amy said. "Call me tonight."

She closed the door and stood very still. Then she

looked at Melissa. "Tasha is one of the people you're sending away?"

Melissa nodded. "You don't care, do you?" She smiled. "And *we're* sending her away. I mean, it's not like you two are friends anymore. Right?"

Amy responded faintly. "Right."

ten 10

Back in his own house, Eric tried to figure out what had just occurred. He'd never seen Amy act that way before. He'd seen her angry, and unhappy, and in a generally bad mood, but he'd never seen her act so strange. Mysterious, almost. It was like she was trying to get rid of him!

He was reminded of something . . . Kyle! That was just how Kyle had acted after he started messing around with Melissa and her clique.

A hard lump formed in Eric's throat. It wasn't possible—was it? The clique had seduced Kyle into becoming one of them. Now it looked like they had managed to do the same thing with Amy. She'd been hanging out with them only because he'd asked her to find out what was going on. But maybe she'd begun to *like* being with them. The way Kyle had.

It was all Eric's own fault. Amy hadn't wanted to get involved. He'd talked her into it. And now he was about to lose her. He sank down on the window seat in the living room, trying to decide what to do.

"What's up with you?" Tasha was on her way out. She paused to look at herself in the mirror that hung over the sofa. "Jealous you weren't chosen as outstanding?"

"You're gorgeous," he said sarcastically. "Now get out of here."

Tasha smiled at him as she sauntered out the front door. He watched her walk down the street and out of sight. Then he glanced toward Amy's house and became lost in thought again.

He hadn't moved when Amy came outside a while later. She wasn't alone.

Eric had asked her to get in with Melissa's clique, but he couldn't believe what he was seeing. Amy was with Melissa. She was with the queen of the clique. He could understand how someone like Jeanine could be infatuated with a supercool glamorous type like Melissa Mitchell. But Amy?

He had to do something. He had to know what they were up to.

Watching from the window, he waited until they turned a corner. Then he bolted out of the house and headed in the same direction.

The school was quiet on this Saturday afternoon, but it wasn't empty. The library was open, and some extra-curricular organizations were holding meetings. But knowing there were others in the building didn't comfort Amy. She couldn't think of any way they could help her out today. In fact, for their own sake, it was probably better if the current occupants stayed as far from the gym as possible.

She could hear the people in the gym before Melissa could. "Jeff is there, setting them up on the risers for the photo," Melissa told her. "The others are meeting us under the bleachers on the left side. We'll go in through the back of the gym so the kids won't see us."

They reached the back gym doors. "Hurry," Melissa whispered to Amy. She ducked in through the doors and hurried under the closest set of bleachers. Amy followed.

No one else from the clique was there. "We must be early," Melissa said. Together they peered through a crack in the bleachers at the students milling around the front of the gym. Amy saw Tasha looking around with a puzzled expression. Amy could hear what Tasha and some of the others were saying.

"Where are we supposed to stand?"

"I don't know, I thought someone would be here."

"Well, I'm not hanging around forever."

Beside her, Melissa was fuming. "I can't believe Jeff's late! I told him to be here at a quarter to one! And where are the others?"

"I think the outstanding nerds are getting impatient," Amy said, still watching the students.

"How do you know?"

"I have good hearing, remember? I told you that."

Melissa looked at her in disbelief. "No one's hearing is *that* good. My hearing is perfect, and I can't make out a thing they're saying."

"Then it's not perfect. I'm telling you, they're going to start leaving if someone doesn't show up soon," Amy reported.

Melissa clenched her fists. "This is unreal. Where *is* everyone?"

"Maybe I should go out and tell them the photographer is late," Amy suggested. "I'll say they have to wait fifteen minutes or something. Maybe more. I mean, they're all a bunch of nerds, so it's not like they have anything better to do with their time."

"That's true," Melissa said.

"Hopefully, the others will show up before too long," Amy added.

"They'd better show up," Melissa said grimly. "Or I'll send *them* away too. Okay, go."

Amy slipped out from behind the bleachers and strode to the front of the gym. Tasha spotted her first. "What are *you* doing here?"

Amy didn't answer. "Could I have everyone's attention, please? Could you all gather around me?" She knew Melissa couldn't hear normal conversation from this distance, but she wasn't going to risk yelling.

As soon as all the students were close enough, Amy spoke. "Everyone has to leave here at once. You're in danger. Get out of the building immediately."

No one moved. Everyone was looking at her like

she was nuts. "What are you talking about?" a boy asked.

"I can't explain now," Amy said softly. "You have to believe me. There's no photographer. You're not out-standing students. It was a trick to get you here! Some-one wants to make you disappear. All of you! Please, please, go! Get out of here!"

The urgency in her voice must have conveyed some-thing real to the students. If nothing else, they proba-bly wanted to get away from *her*. They began to move toward the doors.

"Faster," Amy hissed. "Run!"

They did. But not all of them. Tasha remained in place, and she was glaring at Amy. "Tasha!" Amy knew she was speaking too loudly, but she was too con-cerned to care. "Tasha, get out!"

From behind her, she heard Melissa. "Amy! What are you doing?"

Amy whirled around. Melissa had come out from under the bleachers. "I told them to leave, Melissa."

"But—But you were supposed to tell them to wait. Everyone will be here, they're just late."

"No, they're not late. They're not coming."

"What do you mean? How do you know that?"

"Because I called them all this morning. Blair, Jeff, everyone. It took a little convincing, but they finally believed me when I told them you'd changed the plan. No one's being sent anywhere today, Melissa."

Melissa stared at her. Her eyes became small and hard. "Wanna bet?"

Amy steeled herself to ward off any mental power Melissa might aim in her direction. But Melissa wasn't looking at her anymore. She was looking behind Amy.

Where Tasha was still standing.

"Say bye-bye, Tasha," Melissa sang out.

Amy moved like lightning. Melissa was momentarily stunned by the blur that passed before her eyes as Amy flew across the gym floor to Tasha. Amy pushed Tasha down and threw herself on top of her best friend.

"You think I can't handle both of you?" Melissa shrieked, slowly walking toward them.

Then Amy felt it—a sensation she couldn't even name. It was as if an invisible force had enveloped her body and was pulling her away. As if she was playing tug-of-war—only there was no one on the other end, just an incredibly powerful field of energy.

But Amy was no ordinary person. With every ounce of will she held on, refusing to be dragged off.

She heard Melissa shriek again. For an instant Amy felt the pull loosen, and she turned around. Melissa was on the floor, facedown. Eric was holding her there.

But Melissa wasn't powerless. Tasha screamed, and Amy watched in horror as Eric's body began to rise. He managed to keep one hand on Melissa's neck, pressing her head to the floor, but she was beginning to turn her face toward the row of bleachers. They began to move.

Amy knew what Melissa was trying to do. She was bringing the bleachers closer, closer, until they would all be crushed by the mammoth metal risers. Melissa had to be insane—she would be crushed right along with them. But she obviously didn't care. She kept Eric suspended above her, and the bleachers moved in on them steadily.

Amy rushed forward, and with every ounce of her extraordinary strength, she tried to stop the wall of steel from moving closer. But she knew that her strength had its limits. The tons of steel that made up the bleachers were more than she could handle. Tasha rushed to her side, to help push back the oncoming wall, but her efforts were truly futile.

"Tasha," Amy gasped, panting as she continued to struggle against the metal. "Tasha, I wasn't dumping you for that clique. I was trying to find out what was going on. Eric wouldn't let me tell you because he didn't want to put you in any danger."

"Thanks," Tasha replied breathlessly. "I'd hate to be in danger."

Amy looked over her shoulder. There wasn't much time. "Eric!" she screamed. "I love you!"

"Me too!" squeaked Eric's voice.

Melissa still had her eyes on the bleachers. Then, out of nowhere, Amy was aware of a musical rhythm. It was the throbbing sound of a bass guitar. Suddenly the entire gym was vibrating with the familiar strains of a popular dance hit. Someone had turned on the sound system that was used for school dances. And it had been turned up full blast.

Amy's ears hurt, but another realization struck her immediately. The bleachers had stopped moving. And then she realized what had happened. Melissa's concentration had been broken by the torrent of sound.

Eric fell on top of the screaming girl. Amy and Tasha rushed to join him. Together they dragged Melissa to her feet. She struggled, but the music kept her powerless.

Two men ran in, and one of them slipped what looked like an oxygen mask onto Melissa's face. Almost immediately the girl stopped screaming, her eyes closed, and her body went limp. The men carried her out.

Amy, Tasha, and Eric didn't know what was happening. The music coming from the gym stopped as abruptly as it had started. For a moment all was silent. Then, from behind them, a man spoke.

"In case you're wondering, she'll be taken care of." It was Mr. Devon. "The radioactive ions in her brain will be eliminated, and she'll receive extensive therapy. The others will have no power once her condition has been dealt with."

"What about the kids who disappeared?" Eric demanded.

"They'll be back."

"Are you saying everything will return to normal?" Amy asked.

Mr. Devon didn't respond. He just looked at Amy, then walked out of the gym.

Tasha put her arm around Amy's shoulders. "I don't think I'll complain about school being dull or routine ever again," she said.

Amy smiled. "Better not."

epilogue

Jeanine's face filled the Morgans' television screen. Amy didn't need to use her super-vision to see the tears brimming in her archenemy's eyes.

"What do you remember?" an off-camera voice asked.

"It was terrible," Jeanine whimpered. "One minute I was walking to school. The next, I was in the middle of a forest! I don't know how I got there. I was all alone. I started walking, and I walked for days. I lived on berries and nuts, and I couldn't even wash my hair!"

The camera shifted to the news reporter. "Jeanine's story is similar to the stories we've heard from the two other Parkside Middle School students who disappeared. The exact nature of these disappearances remains a mystery. There is some suspicion that a hallucinogenic narcotic may be responsible for the students' behavior, but all three deny using any drugs. Back to you in the newsroom, Chuck."

Tasha turned off the TV. "I'll bet Jeanine wouldn't mind being lost in a forest every week if she could get this much attention afterward."

"Spence told me that one of those tabloid newspapers called him," Eric said. "They asked if he thinks it might have been an alien abduction."

"You know," Amy mused, "I sort of feel sorry for Melissa. I mean, it wasn't her fault that the radioactive stuff got into her brain."

"Maybe not," Tasha said. "But she loved having the power."

"The whole clique did," Amy agreed. "It was like the ultimate fantasy for them. They could create a whole world of popular kids and send all the uncool ones away."

"Like me," Tasha said mournfully. "I never realized I was considered so uncool."

"Cool has nothing to do with it," Amy assured her. "You were chosen because you told Kristy that Marcy was the best singer in the chorus. She couldn't forgive you for that."

"Wow," Eric said. "They sure know how to hold a grudge."

There was a knock at the Morgans' door, and Eric got up to answer it. "Kyle!"

"Hey, Eric. Thought I'd drop by and see if you want to shoot some hoops."

"Sure."

Amy and Tasha went outside to watch them play. Eric had the ball, and he started dribbling it close to the ground.

"C'mon, Osborne, try to take it!"

Kyle hopped around him, flailing his arms in the air.

"Get in here!" Eric yelled. "Geez, do I have to hand it to you?" That was pretty much what he did. Kyle took the ball and began dribbling awkwardly. The ball bounced away.

"Try again!" Eric yelled.

"Eric," Amy said. "You know when we were in the gym, and the bleachers were closing in on us?"

Eric shuddered. "Don't remind me. Hey, Osborne, focus! Try moving in a straight line, and don't let the ball get away from you!"

"I was wondering," Amy went on. "Remember what we said to each other?"

Eric kept his eyes on Kyle, but Amy didn't miss the hint of red that began to crawl up his neck. "Uh, no, what did we say?"

"Well, I said it first . . . then you said you did too. Remember?"

"I don't know. . . . You said something like 'I feel sick.' And I said 'Me too.' Right?"

Amy sighed. "Yeah, something like that."

"Hey, Morgan!" Kyle yelled. "Watch this!" He stood at the far end of the driveway and threw the ball in the direction of the basket. It didn't even come close.

"That was awful!" Eric declared.

"Really pathetic," Tasha called out.

Kyle just grinned. He didn't look embarrassed at all.

Don't miss the
edge-of-your-seat
Special Edition of

replica

#8

And the Two
Shall Meet

Amy arrives at Wilderness Adventure all pumped up for a week of extreme sports. Her superior strength gives her an edge over the others. But she's ready to rock-climb, mountain-bike, and hang-glide without apologies. Only Eric and Tasha know why things are so easy for her. And Amy is glad they've come along—especially Eric, since she's crazy about him.

But the rugged bonding experience doesn't go exactly as she's planned.

Amy falls for a mysterious guy. Freak accidents abound. Secrets rule.

Soon "extreme" doesn't begin to describe the mad scramble for survival.

Amy's life will change, all right—change forever!

Coming in June!

Official Rules for the

billycrawford

CD & Poster Giveaway

I. ELIGIBILITY:

NO PURCHASE NECESSARY. Enter by printing your name, address, phone number, and date of birth on a 3"x 5" index card and mail to: *Replica*/Billy Crawford CD Offer, Random House Children's Books Marketing Department, 1540 Broadway, 20th floor, New York, NY 10036. Entries must be postmarked no later than May 15, 1999. LIMIT ONE ENTRY PER PERSON. Sweepstakes is open to residents of the United States and Canada, excluding Florida, Rhode Island, Puerto Rico, and the province of Quebec. The winner, if Canadian, will be required to answer correctly a time-limited arithmetic skill question in order to receive the prize. All federal, state, and local regulations apply. Void wherever prohibited or restricted by law. Employees of Random House, Inc., including its parent, subsidiaries, and affiliates; and their immediate families and persons living in their household are not eligible to enter this sweepstakes. Random House is not responsible for lost, stolen, illegible, incomplete, postage-due, or misdirected entries.

II. PRIZES:

Fifty (50) Grand Prizes: Each consists of an "Urgently in Love" Maxi Single and autographed Billy Crawford poster (approximate retail value $50.00 US).

III. WINNERS:

Winners will be chosen in a random drawing on or about June 1, 1999, from all eligible entries received within the entry deadline. Odds of winning depend on the number of eligible entries received. Winners will be notified by mail before June 15, 1999. No prize substitutions are allowed. Taxes, if any, are the winner's sole responsibility. RANDOM HOUSE RESERVES THE RIGHT TO SUBSTITUTE PRIZES OF EQUAL VALUE IF PRIZES, AS STATED ABOVE, BECOME UNAVAILABLE. Winners will be required to execute and return, within 14 days of notification, affidavits of eligibility and release. A noncompliance within that time period or the return of any notification as undeliverable will result in disqualification and the selection of an alternate winner. In the event of any other noncompliance with rules and conditions, prize may be awarded to an alternate winner.

IV. RESERVATIONS:

Entering the sweepstakes constitutes consent to the use of the winner's name, likeness, and biographical data for publicity and promotional purposes by or on behalf of Random House, Inc., with no additional compensation or further permission (except where prohibited by law). Other entry names will NOT be used for subsequent mail solicitation. For the names of the winners, available after June 15, 1999, please send a stamped, self-addressed envelope to: *Replica*/Billy Crawford CD Winners, 1540 Broadway, New York, NY 10036.